COWBOY
HEAT

COWBOY HEAT
WESTERN ROMANCE
FOR WOMEN

EDITED BY
DELILAH DEVLIN

FOREWORD BY
BETH WILLIAMSON

Published in the United States by Cleis Press, Inc., 2246 Sixth Street, Berkeley, California 94710.

Printed in the United States.
Cover design: Scott Idleman/Blink
Cover photograph: Rob Lang/Getty Images
Text design: Frank Wiedemann

First Edition.
10 9 8 7 6 5 4 3 2 1

Trade paper ISBN: 978-1-62778-033-9
E-book ISBN: 978-1-62778-050-6

Contents

FOREWORD

One of the enduring genres in television, films and books is the Western. People have always been fascinated with cowboys. That has not changed in over 150 years, and I don't expect it will anytime soon.

Personally, I have been in love with cowboys since I saw my first Western about forty years ago as a little girl. And when I read my first Western romance? I was HOOKED. Utterly hooked.

One of the questions people often ask me is, "Why do you write Westerns? There are better genres out there."

No, there aren't any better than Westerns! The reason I write them? Because cowboys are my kinda men. Being a cowboy in the nineteenth century was different from being a cowboy today. Yet, the core of the cowboy remains constant. That's what appeals to me, calls to my inner feminine side.

Calloused hands, well-worn jeans, broad shoulders, powerful thighs and the lean-hipped swagger. It's like the secret formula to an addiction I can't control.

What else defines a cowboy? For me, they are like modern-day knights. I know that sounds a bit corny, but let me 'splain. Knights were fierce warriors, but they had a code that set them apart from other men—honor, integrity, dignity and balls of steel.

Cowboys have to be hard, inside and out, but at the same time they feel as deeply as anyone. If not deeper. How could I not write and read stories about cowboys? I fall in love with them from the moment I type their names, feel their hands and hold their hearts in mine.

The stories in this anthology bring you, the reader, on a wild ride. So grab a glass of ice water, settle back and get ready for some cowboy heat.

Beth Williamson
Bestselling author of *Unbridled* and *Hell for Leather*

INTRODUCTION

For years, I lived in the Texas Hill Country, where my ranch-style house was one of many look-alikes in a rural subdivision, with my backyard butted up against a working ranch. After I woke to the insistent mooing of a cow at my bedroom window and her moist breaths fogging the glass, I put up a chain-link fence, which gave me a unique vantage.

My view was panoramic—grassy fields, clumps of wild-flowers, rolling hills, a tall, rugged escarpment in the distance and cowboys riding horses and motorized mules as they herded cattle.

Those cowboys came in all sizes and shapes, but wore "the uniform" well—chambray shirts year round, occasionally torso-hugging T-shirts, if they didn't expect to be in the sun too long, Wranglers (do cowboys wear anything else?) and scuffed, broken-in boots.

And then there was the hat. Those cowboys I watched from my backyard might have worn the same brand of pale, straw cowboy hat, but the brims were shaped according to their individual preferences—some draped low over deep-set eyes, some brims curled tight at the sides to tell you the man wearing it was a little wild and likely playful. If I'd known what I was going to be when I "grew up," I would have learned the language of those hats.

What I did learn was that their muscled frames weren't honed in any gym—cowboys work damn hard. And they take pride in what they are—a living, American icon. Honest, protective and on the side of justice, they walk the walk.

My favorite memories are of strolling down the sidewalk in the small nearby town and passing a tall, lean cowboy coming the other way. Without fail, he'd touch his hat and give me a nod. More often than not, he'd say, "Howdy, ma'am." As corny as that scenario might be, that greeting never failed to make me blush and smile. Back when I wasn't free to act on my attraction, I had my little fantasies. Maybe cowboys made me what I am.

Seems plenty of writers love a sexy cowboy, too. Narrowing down the choices from the deluge of sexy stories I received for this collection was tough. In the end, I selected the stories that turned me on and made me wish I was the girl enjoying her first cowboy. You'll meet rodeo cowboys, Outback jackaroos, cowboys from all over the Western states—all of them turning up the heat on the one girl they can't let go. Enjoy the slow burn.

Delilah Devlin
Central Arkansas

MRS. MORGAN
AND THE
MARSHAL

Emma Jay

S ybil Morgan swung down from the wagon, her skirt and petticoat trailing in the stirred-up dirt of the road outside the general store. She looped the reins over the hitching post and tugged at the waist of her bodice. Wearing a dress was only one reason she hated coming to town. Out on her ranch, she could wear britches and move around with ease, not worrying about getting dirty, getting snagged, being so damned hot.

But a respectable widow had to keep up appearances. She straightened her bonnet and measured her steps so she didn't trip on her skirts as she walked into the general store.

A few townspeople were in the store, which was stifling despite the open doors and windows. Determined to get this chore over with as quickly as possible, she pulled her list out of the pocket in her bodice and waited for the shopkeeper to finish with the other customers. Unaccustomed to standing still, she shifted from one foot to the other.

The air changed and she turned her head to see the town's

marshal, Addison Taylor, in the doorway, removing his hat. He nodded in her direction and she inclined her head in response before turning her attention back to the shopkeeper, who now stood behind the counter with his hand outstretched for her list.

She passed it over. "I'll be back for the supplies in a few hours. I have other errands to attend."

"Yes, Mrs. Morgan."

She turned, head high, and sailed past the marshal, who stepped aside to let her pass before turning to follow her.

"Mrs. Morgan," he said, his voice a low rumble, barely heard above the sound of his boots on the boardwalk. "I'd like to have a word about the recent incidence of rustling on your ranch. Would you mind stepping across the street into my office?"

"Of course," she said, her nipples hardening beneath her confining bodice when he curved his hand beneath her forearm and guided her from boardwalk to dirt street, past riders and other pedestrians. He released her to step ahead and open the door to his office, letting her precede him. When she paused in front of his desk in the empty office, he locked the door behind them, took her hand again and led her into the back and up the stairs to his rooms.

Her heart thundered harder as she absorbed the feel of his rough palm against her bare hand, as she tried to match his determined stride, stumbling on her skirts, damn it.

He tugged her into his apartment over the office, closed the door and latched it in a flurry of movements before he turned to her and loosened her bonnet. He pushed it back from her face so it tumbled to the floor, and curved his hand over her cheek.

"It's been too long," he said softly, and covered her mouth with his.

She bowed into the heat, into the strength of him. She curled her fingers into his shoulders, those broad shoulders she loved to hold. He hadn't shaved, and the prickles of his beard scratched her lips. Instead of pulling back, she pressed closer, parting her lips, welcoming his tongue.

She loved the taste of him, coffee and whiskey and male, loved the slide of his tongue along hers, the intimacy of it. He was skilled at kissing, her marshal, his tongue clever in its knowledge of her mouth, knowing if he touched her there her nipples would ache, and her sex—he called it her pussy, but she had trouble even thinking the word—would grow hot and damp. She could stand here and kiss him all day, savoring the roughness of his unshaven flesh against her tender skin.

He reached between them as he kissed her, and unfastened her bodice, starting at the bottom. She held her breath as if that would help him, but that made kissing difficult.

Her husband had never undressed her, had always waited in the bed for her to join him. They'd never kissed outside of bed, had never touched, not even in the most casual of ways. That her marshal seemed to delight in it delighted her. She stepped back just a bit to let him push the stiff fabric of her bodice off her shoulders, then he closed his hands around her corseted waist. He didn't kiss her again right away, just looked at the way his fingers circled her, almost touching, his hands rough against the silky fabric.

"You don't need this," he murmured in that rough drawl of his.

"Proper ladies wear them whether they need them or not."

His gaze flicked to hers, brown eyes amused. "Is there a proper lady I don't know about under all those clothes?"

She blushed and took a step backward, but he hauled her against him. She'd tried to resist, she had. But one look from him and she lost all sense of propriety, needing only to be in his arms, held by him.

So strange, because she ran her ranch herself since her

husband died, and needed no man. But being with her marshal made her feel safe and secure and cherished—things she hadn't known she needed to feel.

He unlaced the corset, which fastened in front since she had no one to dress her. His movements, combined with the way he looked into her eyes as he loosened the garment and let it fall away, heated her blood. Then his hands slid up her sides, over the damp wrinkled fabric of her chemise, and he stroked his thumbs over her breasts.

She let her eyes flutter shut as he circled her nipples. Her favorite thing, the way he touched her like that, his movements easy and unhurried, as if he didn't know the caresses sent arrows of heat straight to her sex.

He lowered his head and his breath gusted against her skin a moment before he brushed his mouth lightly over her chin, following the line of her jaw back to nuzzle the soft spot beneath her ear.

She whimpered—a sound she only made with him, only made when he was touching her.

He chuckled and brought her closer, his hands spanning her back, her breasts crushed to his chest. She curled her fingers into his hair, holding him to her, guiding him where she wanted his mouth.

He allowed her control for a moment before breaking free and drawing her shimmy off her shoulders, baring her breasts, staring for a long moment before lowering his head to take one dark nipple between his lips.

No, this was her favorite thing, she remembered, as her knees buckled, as her sex swelled and throbbed with need.

"Please, please," she whispered.

He released her nipple with a pop and looked up at her. "Please what?"

She didn't know. Well, she did—she wanted him to touch her sex, to take this horrible hunger for him down to a more manageable level—but at the same time, the anticipation was delicious.

"Don't stop," was all she managed.

He bent his head again and blew a cool breath over her damp nipple. It tightened so much it ached, but instead of appeasing her, he turned his head to her other breast.

As he suckled her, he reached up and pulled the pins from her hair, letting the heavy mass fall down her back. The cool sensation of it against her naked shoulders and back was almost as arousing as his mouth at her breast, because she knew soon it would be the only thing she was wearing.

He unfastened her skirt with one twist of his fingers. The garment caught on the width of her petticoats, which he untied without looking. The fabric pooled at her feet, leaving her in her shimmy, stockings and boots. He lifted her from amid the puddle and carried her to his bed, lowering her to the mattress and sliding down her body to push her shimmy up and unfasten her cotton stockings. He held her gaze as he rolled them down, his hands rough on the sensitive skin of her thigh. Her shallow breathing only made him take his time, caressing every inch of her leg before disposing of one stocking and turning his attention to the other one.

"Aren't you a picture?" he murmured once the garments were tossed aside. He slid his hands up her legs, pushing the shimmy so it bunched at her middle. His fingers rested lightly on her hips as he looked at her sex, then pressed a light kiss to the inside of her knee.

Everything in her began to quiver. The last time they'd been together, he'd coaxed her legs apart and kissed her there, shaming her, initially, but in the days that followed, she could think of nothing but the pleasure he'd given her with his mouth, his tongue. And he'd taken pleasure in it, too. That had surprised her as much as anything.

Feeling a little bold, she parted her legs in invitation. He chuckled and glided his hand across her belly to stroke the curls cloaking her sex. She pressed her tongue to the roof of her mouth as heat flooded her channel. She could feel her wetness in her folds.

"Ah, god, Sybil." His voice was choked and his eyes were hot.

She parted her thighs wider and could smell her own musk. Her head swam with desire, and she had to ask. "Will you kiss me there again?"

"Kiss you where?" His smile canted, so handsome he made her heart hurt. "Here?" He pressed his lips to the inside of her knee, in the same spot he'd kissed before.

"Higher."

He slid between her parted knees, his body hot and hard, and kissed her inner thigh, letting his stubble rasp the tender skin. She bit her lower lip against a keening cry.

"Higher."

He lifted himself over her and kissed below her navel. She twisted in frustration, hooking her feet on his belt to push him down.

"Lower."

His lips slid over her belly, just above her curls. "Tell me what you want, Sybil."

No one called her Sybil anymore. Even her husband hadn't. And she loved the way it sounded on his lips, gentle despite the roughness of his voice. Tender.

Dear heaven, was she falling in love with this man? That wasn't supposed to happen. This was an arrangement for two independent people who didn't need love, didn't need marriage.

"Kiss me. Between my legs."

"On your..." He trailed his voice off, leading her.

"On my...puss." She thought her face would burst into flames as she said the word, looking into his eyes.

He smiled and lowered his head, his thumbs parting her, and then a flick of his tongue over her tender flesh sent her bowing into him. He repeated the caress, sliding one hand under her bottom to hold her still. Her entire being focused on the movement of his mouth on her slick petals, the circling of his tongue, the heat of his breath, each caress building, building, winding around in her. She didn't realize her hands were twisted in his hair, holding him to her, until he reached up to loosen them. Then he pressed her legs open farther, focusing on the little nub he'd helped her discover, flicking and sucking until she couldn't breathe, couldn't see.

She climaxed with a cry that might have been heard all the way down Main Street, but she didn't care as waves of pleasure rolled through her, loosening her muscles, her inhibitions.

He lifted his head and looked at her. "I love to watch you come."

Come. That was what he called her climax. Orgasm, too, was another word he'd taught her. And fuck. She'd been so sheltered until she met him, until she'd allowed him into her bed. She hadn't known she was made like this, made for passion, until she met him.

She closed her legs when he shifted to lie on his side, fully dressed beside her. "Is there something I can do to you that brings the same pleasure?"

His eyes darkened, the passion in them almost frightening. "You can lick my cock."

She frowned. "And that feels as good to you?"

"It can. Or you can put it in your mouth."

She mentally recoiled. How could she...oh, no. *No, no, no, no, no.* But twice he'd put his mouth where she'd never expected, and she owed it to him to try. She rose on her elbow and began unbuttoning his shirt.

He allowed it, watching her face, which meant she kept her gaze on the buttons, and on the skin she bared. She ran her palm over the light fur covering his chest, a delicious sensation. Then with his help, she pushed the garment from his shoulders. Regaining some of her boldness, she kissed his shoulder, brushing her lips back and forth over the cap of muscle, feeling it bunch beneath her mouth. She followed her instincts, her own pleasure, and trailed her lips across his collarbone, down the center of his chest, feeling his breath hitch with each inch she moved.

Something about that, about having that effect on him, made her feel powerful, and she rose to unfasten his belt. Her fingers faltered a bit, but she managed before he had to come to her aid. She pushed his pants down just enough to free his thick cock. Just thinking the word had her blushing.

He was hard and long and arching toward her, as if understanding what she meant to do. She rubbed her tongue against the roof of her mouth for a moment, then bent to lightly swipe it across the head of him.

His groan echoed in the small room, so she did it again. He reached down to close his fingers around himself.

"Right here," he said huskily, pointing to an arrow of flesh beneath the thicker head. "Lick there."

She did, hesitantly, with the point of her tongue, then again, with the flat of it. The taste of him wasn't unpleasant, and the scent of him was arousing, concentrated. She licked again, then changed her angle to guide him into her mouth, parting her lips wide.

He tensed his stomach, his thighs, his hips, as if he was holding himself back. "More," he rasped, and she did her best to comply, easing her way with her tongue along his shaft.

The sound that ripped from him was barely human, and she felt his muscles quivering, his pulse hot and fast against her tongue. She felt suddenly very powerful, and opened her mouth wider to take more of him.

"Up and down," he urged. "My god, Sybil."

She did as he asked, mimicking what she thought it must feel like to be inside her channel, bobbing her head, sliding her tongue. His hands fisted in her hair, guiding her movements before he pushed her away, leaving her mouth swollen and empty.

He rose from the bed and shed his pants with an economy of movement, then dropped back over her, parting her knees with his hips, parting her lower lips with the head of his cock before driving into her.

They both cried out as he plunged in to the hilt. He cupped the back of her head and pulled her up, covering her mouth with his in a carnal kiss, giving her a taste of herself on his lips and tongue, absorbing his own taste from her mouth. She wound her arms around his neck, returning his kiss, and wound her legs around his hips, holding him to her, deep inside her.

Then he began to move, his cock caressing the depth of her channel, stretching her so that every nerve inside her felt exposed, aroused. His hips flexed, each movement powerful, each thrust, each withdrawal exciting her. His body pressed rhythmically against the nub that focused her passion, and she bumped against him with each plunge, driving her own desire higher.

They found their rhythm, reaching together for the pleasure

they could only find with each other. He rose over her to look into her eyes as he made love to her, as he reached between their bodies to find the nub with his rough thumb, to circle it, flick it until...

"Oh!" She pushed up against him as the orgasm swamped her, tightening everything in her before sending her spiraling in long, deep pulses.

The contraction of her orgasm tightened her channel around him rhythmically, pulling on him, and her legs tightened on his hips. With a shout, he broke free, pulling out of her and coming on her stomach in hot wet streaks.

He collapsed beside her, one arm crooked over his eyes, the other tightening around her, pulling her to his side, unmindful of the mess he'd just made. When he caught his breath, he brought her close for a long, deep kiss.

"We should get married," he murmured when the kiss ended.

The tension that had washed from her body with her climax, with his kiss, returned triple-fold, and she pulled away, rolling off the bed to deal with the mess. "I've no desire to marry again, to give any power to a man."

"You give me power every time you come to my bed," he said, rolling onto his side, not appearing the least bit offended.

"And you give it to me."

"What's to say that wouldn't carry on in our marriage?"

"Because that's not the way of the world." She wiped her stomach with a rough towel dipped in water from the basin near the window.

"Sybil, we're in Texas. The ways of the world don't matter much here. You know that better than anyone." He rose and stood behind her, wrapping his arms around her and pulling her back against his chest.

She loved it when he held her like this, loved his strength

and his heat and his tenderness. But not enough to give over the control of her ranch, her life.

"I'll never forget the first time I saw you, riding hell-for-leather after those rustlers. At first I thought you were just a kid." He cupped her breasts briefly and smiled against her neck. "Never was I so glad to have my powers of observation fail me."

She remembered his surprise so well, first anger, then grudging admiration for a woman who took matters into her own hands. He'd joined her in her search for the rustlers, though she knew he'd wanted to send her home. She'd proved to him she could take care of herself, and anything else that came along, and saw the shift in his attitude.

And when he'd kissed her for the first time out on the trail of the bandits, well, she had let him. Who was she fooling? She'd loved it, and everything else he'd done to her. But was she ready for something more permanent?

"Don't you want to stop waiting for a month to see each other? To stop sneaking around? To have children?" He curved his hand over her belly. "I would love for you to be the mother of my children. They'd be fierce and strong and loving."

His words made her heart trip. She had thought about children—after all, why work so hard on the ranch if she had no one to pass it to? And children with him—why should the idea of growing large with his baby send this rush of pleasure through her, a pleasure almost as strong as when his body was inside hers?

Because she was in love with him. But she could never tell him, could never give him that ammunition. As soon as he knew that, he'd never give up on this crazy desire to marry.

"I need to go. Mr. Damien will be waiting for me."

"We haven't had lunch yet."

"I need to get back." She wouldn't meet his gaze. "There's so much to do." She broke free of his embrace, though it pained her to do so, and went about the business of getting dressed.

She was perfectly presentable when she walked back into the general store to pay for her supplies. It wasn't until she was on the road to the ranch that she burst into tears.

A little over a week had passed since she made her escape from Addison and his proposition. She couldn't exactly call it a proposal, could she? He hadn't asked her to marry him, just stated that they should. And while she dreamed at night of waking up beside him, of corralling their children—she thought maybe three, God willing—she had fought long and hard for this ranch and was damned if she'd hand it over to a man who could do as he pleased with it.

She didn't know what she'd do, exactly, when she went back to town, if she'd act like the conversation never took place, or if she'd ignore him completely. But at the same time, she didn't want to cut him out of her life. She would just make him see the arrangement they had was the best all around.

One of her hands gave a shout and she stepped out of the barn to see two riders approaching the ranch, one tall in the saddle on a roan horse she recognized, the other shorter and clearly uncomfortable on the back of the paint pony.

She wiped her hands on her britches, her heart thundering. Addison never came out here, even when she'd had the rustling trouble. What could have gone wrong? She moved to the gate to meet them, trying to read Addison's expression as he rode toward her. He nodded at her and touched his hat, a respectful gesture that belied the heated look in his eyes as he took in her attire.

"Mrs. Morgan, would it be possible for us to speak in the house?"

She looked from him to the stranger and lifted a brow.

"This is Mr. Cavanaugh, a lawyer from San Antonio."

A lawyer? Nerves dancing along the outside of her skin, she motioned for the two men to ride toward the house while she followed on foot. She watched Addison dismount with easy grace not echoed by his lawyer friend, then pumped fresh water into the trough by the hitching post.

"A lawyer, Marshal?" she asked, not allowing her voice to show her nervousness.

"We'll speak inside," he said, removing his hat and gesturing with it to the house.

Mind whirling at the possibilities, she led the way into the house and into the sitting room, where she offered both men a seat. The lawyer took her up on it; Addison didn't. Instead, he drilled her with those whiskey-brown eyes. She held his gaze for a long moment, but then he looked past her out the window.

He cleared his throat. "After our last conversation, I decided to consult a lawyer. I had a hard time finding one who would do what I wanted, which is why I haven't been out before today. Mr. Cavanaugh here is from San Antonio because every other lawyer told me he couldn't create this." He turned back to Sybil. "What we have here is a contract, legally binding, saying I want no part of this ranch, that you will have the final say as long as you're living, and that you and any children we might have will be in total control."

"Any...children?"

He stepped forward and grabbed her hands in his.

She realized she still wore her work gloves, and his hands were bare. She wanted to feel his touch but didn't want to remove her gloves in front of the lawyer, and thus draw attention to her rough ways.

"I love you, Sybil, and I want to marry you and have a life

with you, a family. If this ranch is in the way, well, I won't let it be. And now it's not. It's yours, and we have the contract to prove it."

He turned to the lawyer, who held the piece of paper and a pen. Addison released her hands and took the pen, signing his name with short, spastic movements. Then he knelt on one knee.

"Sybil Morgan, I just signed away any claim or rights to this land in order to win your hand in marriage. I want to go to bed with you, wake up with you, grow old with you. I want you to be the strong and brave mother of my children. I love you. Will you marry me?"

Since he'd made his announcement, she couldn't catch her breath. He'd done this for her, so she would retain control? So the ranch would never come between them? How did she deserve a man like this, so giving and so appealing? She looked down into his eyes and saw he was holding his breath as he waited for her answer.

"Yes, Addison, I'll marry you."

He rose then and cupped her face in his hands to kiss her, a very improper kiss in front of the lawyer, who cleared his throat.

Addison drew back, his fingers stroking her wild hair back from her face. She looked into his beloved eyes and said the words she never thought she'd say, never thought she'd feel.

"I love you."

REMEMBER

Mia Hopkins

*There will come a time when you believe everything
is finished; that will be the beginning.*
—Louis L'Amour

Eliza was almost through her first bottle when the phone
rang. She checked the number before answering.

Penny, Eliza's maid of honor, didn't waste time with hello.
"Should I come over? We can get takeout and watch old movies."

Eliza sat down on the floor, still clutching the neck of the
bottle. "No. It's all right."

"Have you even gotten out of bed today?"

"I went to the gym a couple of hours ago," Eliza said. "I even
showered. I'm just dandy. No need to worry."

"So what are you doing?"

"Drinking the wine. All of it. 'Til I pass out."

"Jesus. Two hundred bottles. Can't you return them?"

Eliza looked at the stacks of boxes in her living room and

took another swig. "No," she said. "He wanted custom labels. 'Eliza and Ryan, Today I Marry My Best Friend.'" She sighed. "At least it's good cabernet."

"Sure you don't want company?"

"I'm fine."

"Tonight was supposed to be your bachelorette party. We should do something involving alcohol. Alcohol and promiscuity."

Wine fumes swirled in Eliza's head. "Well," she said. "I've got the alcohol part covered. After that I'm going to bed. You go be promiscuous tonight."

"Eliza, you take care of yourself. I'll come round tomorrow and we'll go to brunch. Okay, sweetie?"

"Okay." Eliza put down the phone and stood up slowly, putting her hand on the wall to steady herself. After another swig, the bottle was empty. She plunged her hand into the nearest box for another. She opened it, took a swallow, and lay down on the floor.

Eliza had been hiding out for two days, ever since she'd come home to an empty apartment and a letter from her fiancé. The wedding was supposed to have been in a week, but Ryan had run off with his ex-girlfriend as though his relationship with Eliza had been nothing but an ill-advised fling.

The doorbell rang. Eliza staggered up to open it, the wine bottle still in her hand. She was wearing a T-shirt, yoga pants, and a messy ponytail. "I told you not to come over, Penny," she said, opening the door.

"Excuse me, miss," said the stranger. His voice was a deep drawl. "Is this Apartment B?"

Eliza put the bottle down on the hallway table and turned on the porch light. The man was wearing a white cowboy hat; his face was still in shadow.

"Um, yes. Who are you?"

Well over six feet with long legs and a broad chest, he cast a big shadow over Eliza, whose eyes widened as she looked him over. Jeans, chaps, cowboy boots and a sleeveless flannel shirt that showed off arms that were manifestations of the diagrams in her old nursing textbooks. And he was carrying a boom box.

"I'm here for Eliza, the bride-to-be. I believe Penny's arranged a party for her."

Oh, Jesus, thought Eliza. *She forgot to cancel the stripper.*

He tipped his hat back, inadvertently flexing his bicep and revealing the most incredible eyes Eliza had ever seen. They were sky blue, but half of the iris of his right eye was brown shot through with shards of gold. *Heterochromia*, thought Eliza. Eyes of different colors. As if God couldn't make up His mind.

Her skin began to tingle under his gaze.

"Are you Penny?" he asked.

Once, after watching *Butch Cassidy and the Sundance Kid* over chow mein, Eliza had mentioned to Penny that she thought cowboys were sexy.

"Cowboys? Really?" Penny had asked. "But you're such a city girl."

"I know," she'd replied. "There's just...something about cowboys."

Like she always had, Penny stored that tidbit of information away, waiting for the opportune moment to use it. Mr. Opportune Moment flexed his jaw as he squinted at Eliza. Five o'clock shadow shaded his perfect cleft chin. "Wait, are you Eliza?" he asked, taking a step forward.

Eliza thought wine was supposed to dull the senses, but as he came toward her, his scent filled her nose. Sagebrush and pine, but also something more elusive: leather. His own skin. He smelled like sex. Eliza breathed deep.

"Um," she said, blocking his way and nearly colliding with his chest. "The party's been canceled. I'm sorry."

"Rescheduled?"

"No. The wedding's off," she said.

He stood so close to her that she could feel the heat rising off his arms. "But...you're Eliza, right?" he asked.

"Yes."

"Hmm." Again his gaze raked over her.

Her body tightened in response.

"Listen, Eliza," he said slowly. "Your friend's already paid me in full, and I've got no other appointments tonight. I can still dance for you. If you're up for it."

"Let me guess. You have a no-refunds policy?"

"Something like that," he said.

"And you dance for one person at a time?"

"Sometimes," he said with a smirk.

He was all kinds of handsome. She was all kinds of heart-broken. Eliza reached back and picked up the bottle of wine again and took a drink to give her courage. Then she opened the door wide and let him in. "What the hell," she muttered.

Heaven help her, he sauntered right in.

"Do you want a drink?" she asked, closing the door.

"Got any whiskey?" he asked. He put his boom box down on the coffee table and sized up the room.

"No," she said. "But I've got red wine. Lots of it."

"Red wine gives me a headache," he said. He looked at all the boxes.

"And whiskey doesn't?"

"I like the kind of headache whiskey gives me." He turned off the overhead light and switched on a small lamp on the mantle. "Can I move this?" he asked, indicating an armchair that she had set up next to the window.

"Sure," she said, then watched with fascination as he hauled up the sturdy chair as though it weighed nothing. He set it down carefully in the middle of the room.

"What's your name?" she asked.

"Chase," he said.

"Is that your real name?"

"Nope," he said, smiling. He sat down in the chair and bounced as if to make sure it was comfortable. "But I'll tell you my real name if you tell me something."

"What?"

"Who left whom at the altar?"

She wasn't expecting the question, but something about his manner made her feel at ease. "He left me," she said.

"Did you see it coming?"

"No," she said. "Not at all."

"How long were you together?"

"Four years."

"How old are you anyway?"

"I'm twenty-three." He squinted at her, and she put the bottle down. "My turn," she said. "What's your real name?"

"Chase."

She rolled her eyes. "Sure. And the accent? Fake or real?" she asked.

"Real."

"Texas?"

"Tennessee," he said. "Born and bred. And I'm not a cowboy. I'm a hillbilly. There's a difference."

"So...hillbillies wear chaps?"

"They do when they're strippin'." He stood up and walked toward her. "Shall we start, Eliza?"

"No, I have more questions," she said, putting her hands on her hips.

He raised an eyebrow. "Okay, beautiful, fire away."

He'd called her *beautiful*. "Are you gay?" she asked.

"No," he said. "Very straight."

"Why are you stripping?"

"Because I need to eat. Between auditions."

"Ah, a starving actor," she said.

"I'm not starving at all." He smirked again, infuriatingly handsome. "What do you do?"

"I'm a nurse at the V.A.," she said.

"No problem, then," he said. "Gorgeous girl like you? Forget about your ex and find yourself a nice soldier boy."

She ignored the gorgeous comment. "Not the ones who come to the V.A."

"Why not?"

"The only reason a young guy goes to the doctor is because he has some kind of venereal disease."

"That can't be true," he scoffed.

"Oh, yeah? When was the last time you went to the doctor?"

He cocked his head. "Last week."

"Why?"

"To make sure I *don't* have VD. And I was right." He took two more steps toward her. "Being a nurse and all, you don't have to take my word for it. You can examine me yourself."

Eliza's cheeks felt feverish, and not just from the wine. He held out his hand. "Are you ready now?" he asked.

She looked at the big hand he offered her and took it. It was hard and warm. "Okay."

"Then set yourself down in that chair, beautiful."

She knew the song from the country radio station: "Crazy Town." The electric guitars were joined by licks from a fiddle, and then the twang of Jason Aldean's voice. Her cowboy started out with his back to her, Wranglers wrapped around a truly breathtaking ass.

"Nice," she said, slurring. "I thought you would've gone with something more predictable, like 'Save a Horse, Ride a Cowboy.'"

"Hush," he said. "I'm working."

He spun around and moved his hips in time to the music. He lowered his hat over his eyes and looked down, hiding his face from her and forcing her to look at his body. His broad forearms were lined with a few faint veins. He hooked his thumbs over his belt and spun around again, moving backward until he was straddling her lap; his ass was in her face. As he shook it, she covered her mouth to suppress a giggle.

He reached behind him, grabbed both of her hands, and placed them high on his chest. Through his shirt she could feel how hard his muscles were. *Some pectoralis major*, she thought. *Jesus.*

As the music bumped on, he moved her hands slowly down his body. When her palms slid over his abs, she felt as though she were feeling up a river rock wall.

Before she knew what was happening, he'd turned around to look at her face-to-face. He took off his hat and flung it away, revealing a head of wavy dark hair. He picked up her hand again and ran it through that mink-soft hair. In spite of a brain that was addled by wine and disbelief, her body responded to him, and she felt her core temperature rise to scalding.

He took her hands and placed them on his granite asscheeks. "Keep 'em there, beautiful," he said.

What was happening? She had no idea. He pulled his shirt open with one swift move and pulled it out of his jeans in time with the music. He threw it aside and Eliza had nowhere else to look but at his bare chest just inches from her face.

Without waiting for him to prompt her, she ran her left hand from his pecs over his rigid six-pack. Her thumb stopped in the hollow of his belly button. Her mouth went dry.

"Lie down for me," he murmured.

He took her hands and helped her up. He pushed the chair out of the way, took the hat off her head, and laid her down on the floor facing up.

The song ended and faded into "Save a Horse, Ride a Cowboy."

"I knew it!" She laughed.

"What? It's a classic," he said with a smirk. He stood above her, untied a leather lace, and threw off his fringed chaps. Underneath, his jeans were soft and worn and stretched tight across hard quads. He got down on his knees, straddling her hips, and began to undulate over her. The slide of muscles underneath his skin was hypnotic. As he wove back and forth, he kept his eyes locked on hers.

Then he got into a push-up position above her. The music from the boom box blasted in her ears. Where his chest brushed hers, she felt her skin burning. Her nipples hardened against her T-shirt.

"You're going to think I'm lying, Eliza," he said, "but I think you're sexy as hell. Your fiancé's a damn fool."

She looked at the face above hers. "Are you joking?" she asked.

"Nope," he said. His voice dropped even deeper. "Can I kiss you?"

She blinked. "What?"

"Let me kiss you, Eliza."

Still not sure if she was awake or dreaming, she gave him a small nod.

Then he was kissing her. His lips were full and firm. He turned slightly and covered her mouth with his. When a long moan of longing escaped from Eliza's throat, he smiled against her lips.

"I've wanted to do that ever since you opened the door."

The music stopped abruptly, and Eliza felt as though she were in freefall. She could hear him breathing as she reached up and stroked his back, discovering muscles she didn't know existed.

He dipped his head and kissed her harder, licking into her mouth with the tip of his tongue.

Her nerve endings fired like rocket blasters as he picked her up and carried her to the bedroom.

"What are you doing?" she asked.

"You know what I'm doing," he said. "Question is, do you want me to do it?"

She tucked her head against his jaw and breathed him in.

"Eliza," he said, laying her on the bed. "You've gotta say it, or I won't touch you."

She tried to focus her gaze on him. His torso was a landscape of deep canyons and rounded hills.

"Tell me what you want me to do." He leaned over her.

The alcohol in her bloodstream had been replaced with adrenaline. Stone-cold sober, she licked her lips and said, "Help me forget."

"No, Eliza. I'll help you remember," he said. He kissed her again, long and deep.

The fire spread from her lips down to her thrumming clit. "Remember what?" she whispered.

"What it feels like being free." He began to take his belt off.

"No tear-away pants?" she asked.

"Not for the cowboy getup," he said, dropping the heavy buckle. "I don't usually take the jeans off."

Eliza watched as he unbuttoned his fly and slid down his pants, revealing tight gray boxer-briefs. Before she could see what kind of heat he was packing, he turned away and sat on the edge of the bed. The mattress springs snapped under his weight as he pulled off his boots.

He turned to her and stroked her arm with the back of his knuckle. "Pretty young thing," he whispered. "How many guys have you slept with?"

Why didn't she feel uncomfortable telling him? "One," she said.

He whistled, long and low. "Too bad. Looks like you dropped your basket."

"What basket?"

"The one holding every one of your eggs."

Before she could respond, he put his lips on hers again, this time freely swirling his tongue into her mouth.

She sat up, holding on to his massive shoulders as though she would spin off the Earth if she let go. He pulled her T-shirt over her head and undid her ponytail. Her hair tumbled down and goose bumps rose on her skin. He reached behind her, unhooked her bra and slid it forward, off her shoulders.

She loved how he handled her.

He laid her back, and then kissed her neck and collarbone, slowly making his way down her body. "Beautiful," he whispered against her skin, cupping her breasts in his big hands. He ran his hot tongue around the areola of her left nipple and sucked her up between his lips.

The heat of him knifed through her; her pussy watered like a mouth. He stroked and pinched and licked and sucked. The scrape of his stubble put her senses on overload, and every time he ran his tongue over her nipples she felt tremors shiver between her legs.

He pulled down her leggings and panties and dropped them on the floor. He climbed onto the bed and spread her legs, cupping the backs of her knees and bending them so that he could get a good look at her.

Eliza turned her head away in embarrassment. Her whole body flushed pink while he fixed his heterochromatic gaze on her sex, then melted when he turned on the nightstand lamp so he could see while he parted her with his fingers, exposing her to the kiss of cool air.

"Look at that pretty pussy," he said, his voice deepening. "Goddamn. You're beautiful." He made a V with his fingers and gently spread her open and then glanced up. "What?" he asked. "Are you embarrassed? He never looked at you like this?"

Mutely, she shook her head.

"If you were mine, I'd look at you all day, every day. Pussy like this? I'd never leave the house." He got down on his forearms until his face was an inch or two from her.

Her heart tapped like a flamenco dancer, and all the breath left her lungs when with his hot tongue, he gave her one long lick from her perineum to the tip of her clit.

He gave her a crooked grin, and then wrapped his arms around her waist and carried her higher up the bed, resting her ass on a stack of pillows. When she leaned back, her hips jutted upward, her pussy high in the air.

He rested his hands on her inner thighs and spread her farther. Then he dipped his head and kissed her long and deep where she needed it most, lapping at her and making her body weep with pent-up longing. He sucked on her, drinking in the juices of her arousal, his eyes closing as though he were having a cool drink of water on a hot summer day.

Then he released her with a wet smack. "Jesus Christ," he muttered. He began to stroke her. Slowly, he held a fingertip right at her opening, tracing the delicate rim and driving her insane. Then he put the thumb of his other hand on her clit and began to trace tiny circles on that pinhead of packed nerves. He slid a long finger into her and curled it slightly, immediately finding the sweet spot her ex had never found.

Her toes curled into the sheets. She threw her head back and moaned.

"That's it," he said. He began to move his hand back and forth, thrusting into her heat and summoning thunderheads of pleasure she felt gathering on the horizon.

He replaced his thumb with his tongue and was soon strumming her clit with a slow, steady rhythm.

She tightened, feeling as though he were gathering all her loose nerve endings, weaving them into a thick rope that he was about to yank. Hard.

With each minute that passed, she felt the tension in her body swirl and intensify. The pillowcase under her ass was soaked with her hot juices; she was trembling and twitching, her back arched in complete surrender to his gifted tongue.

Suddenly, he stopped.

She gasped, arrested at the edge.

"Squeeze your tits." His voice had a rough edge to it, making it even sexier than before. "Pinch those pretty pink nipples."

She did as he told her. For once, she let herself feel how smooth and heavy her breasts felt in her own hands. She rubbed her nipples, then pinched them until they were as hard as diamonds.

He easily slid a second finger into her wet pussy, opening her up and making her clit throb angrily against the tip of his tongue. Then he began to fuck her hard and fast with his fingers. He quickened his rhythm on her clit, pulling the hood back with the fingers of his other hand and flicking his tongue against the hypersensitive tip.

She felt as if the whole world were falling apart around her. "I'm—going to—holy shit," she stammered.

He drove his tongue against the naked glans of her clit and

she came. Her pelvic bones crackled with the force of her climax; he held her legs open and feasted on her as she shuddered wetly into his mouth.

When she was finished, he stood up from the bed and slid out of his boxers. He walked toward her, six foot three of sinuous muscle, his eyes ablaze with lust.

Battered and weak, Eliza let him pick her up again and set her on the dressing table. He ran his hands up her inner thighs as she stared, transfixed by his enormous cock. Three inches longer than Ryan's, it was nearly as thick as her wrist.

He took it in his hand and gave it a quick stroke, smearing some of her juices over its glistening pink head. "Like what you see?" he asked.

A drop of fresh liquid seeped out of her pussy. She reached for him.

Rigid and hot, he jerked against her palm. His balls were as big as peaches.

"You're huge," she said.

"And you're tight. How're we gonna manage?" he said. His voice was husky and ragged. He grabbed the base of his cock and swirled the head slowly over her swollen labia and clit.

She grabbed onto his shoulders to steady herself.

Again he captured her lips with his, swallowing her gasp of surprise and making her taste her own pussy juices where they lingered on his tongue.

Without breaking the kiss, he grabbed her ass. With one deft movement, he slid the head of his cock into her, thrust in an inch, then pulled back again, thrusting deeper the next time, letting her wetness coat his shaft as the tender tissues of her sex stretched painfully around him.

"Jesus Christ," he gasped. "You have one sweet little cunt, Eliza." She clenched at the dirty word, and he groaned. "Do that again," he said, looking into her eyes, "and I don't think I'll be able to hold back."

"I don't want you to," she said, clenching.

His eyes narrowed. He pulled out of her almost completely then flexed his ass and gave her one, smooth thrust, carving into her flesh and burying himself inside her deeper than she'd ever been fucked before.

They moaned together at the exquisite pain and pleasure that washed over them like a douse of ice water followed by hot. And just when Eliza thought the feeling couldn't get any better, he thrust again, three more inches of hot cock filling up a space inside her she hadn't known existed.

He was inside her to the hilt before he leaned in and kissed her again. "My real name is Tyler," he whispered.

As if set free, he began to fuck her good and deep. With each thrust, his ass flexed in her hands and pleasure spiked straight up her spine, overloading her brain with sensation. The perfume bottles on her dressing table clinked together as if toasting her good fortune.

With a grunt, he picked her up once more and slammed her against the wall, digging even deeper. He kissed her neck and kneaded her ass where he held her. He slid his hand between them and immediately found her clit, swirling the pad of his middle finger on it until she felt another orgasm rising.

"I think you want to come again," he growled, still plucking at her clit. He picked her legs up as he plowed away at her.

Eliza trembled around him, stuck between a steel-bodied man and the cold wall behind her.

Tyler groaned and closed his eyes. His scent mingled with hers; the bedroom smelled like distilled sex.

Abruptly, he put her back on the bed and pulled out of her. "Get on your hands and knees," he demanded.

She did so, and he dragged her backward until her hips were at the edge of the bed. He reached for his jeans, pulled out a condom, and rolled it on.

"Spread yourself open, Eliza. Let me see that delicious cunt."

He was all cowboy and all man. When she did it, he thrust his tongue into her pussy, and she cried out. Then he shoved his cock inside her and began riding her hard. Their bodies smacked together, flesh against muscle. He straightened up and dug the head of his cock against the front wall of her pussy.

"Oh god," she gasped.

He pushed her shoulders down until she was leaning on her forearms, her ass high in the air. He grabbed her hair in one fist and pulled her head back, then reached around her hip with his other hand and began to rub at her tender clit. He was slamming into her; the pleasure he gave her was cut with pain. His cock was enormous. His touch was no longer gentle.

But she needed what he was giving her. She needed it like she needed air to breathe. "Yes," she rasped. At once, her body went supernova. Her pussy gnawed hard at his cock with each excruciating convulsion. But he kept fucking her. He didn't stop, even as she came raw and hard around him.

"Let it out," he said, almost soothingly.

He thrust into her as deeply as he could, slapping his heavy balls against her pussy lips and sliding her up and down his shaft as though she were his own personal sex toy.

"I'm coming," he gasped. His fingers bit into her flesh. All of his muscles flexed at once, gloriously, as his orgasm ripped through him. She bent backward to look at him. His wild blue-brown eyes fixed on hers as he shuddered and emptied himself into her in sweet silence.

* * *

When Eliza woke up, Tyler was gone. He'd left a business card on her nightstand, the only evidence that she hadn't dreamed him up.

Rising from her hangover, she took a long bubble bath to soothe her sore muscles. Penny came to pick her up at ten and they drove to their favorite coffee shop.

"You look a lot better today," said Penny over pancakes. "Did you finally get a good night's sleep?"

"Well," said Eliza. "Yes, actually." She pursed her lips. "But...I think you forgot to cancel the stripper."

Realization dawned on Penny's face. "Shit. I'm sorry. I called all the girls and took care of the caterer. But the dancer just slipped my mind."

"No, it was fine," said Eliza. "*He* was fine, too."

"You let him dance for you?" laughed Penny. "I knew you had a wild streak in you."

I let him do a lot more than dance for me, thought Eliza. "At least your money didn't go to waste," she said.

"What?" asked Penny.

"He said you'd already paid him."

"No, I didn't."

Eliza put down her fork. "Are you sure?"

"Positive," said Penny, grinning. "I didn't give him a single cent."

After Penny had dropped her off, Eliza picked up Tyler's business card from the nightstand. It read, *Chase Woodcock, Entertainer, LA Studs*. She snorted at his stage name and flipped the card over. On the back he had written his personal phone number and the message, *For Eliza. From Tyler. Remember.*

As if she would ever forget.

COWBOY
DOWNTIME

Cheyenne Blue

He was leaning against the fence watching as she led her mare out of the float.

Mel's skin prickled into awareness, every nerve fired up by his presence. Ignoring him, she tied Minty to the rail and clomped back up the ramp to get her grooming kit. When she returned, he was standing with one hand on her horse's neck, his hard-muscled body relaxed and at ease.

Mel grabbed the dandy brush and advanced on her horse.

Jack's hand dropped, but he didn't move.

"Excuse me," she clipped.

His lazy smile stretched wide. "Don't let me get in your way."

"Then shift your arse."

He moved fractionally, but remained close enough that she fancied she could feel the heat emanating from his broad chest.

Mel concentrated on her horse, hissing softly through her teeth, although it was more to soothe her own twitching nerves than for Minty.

"Ready for the game?" Jack asked, seemingly unconcerned by her prickly attitude. "Ready for a thrashing?"

"I wouldn't call it that," she flung back, goaded by his words. "We beat you fair and square last time. Guess we had the better attack. What was the score again? Oh yeah, fifteen to twelve."

Methodically, she worked down Minty's forelegs, removing the dust of the journey.

"Remains to be seen if you'll be better this time."

"I'll always beat you, Jack Mitchell," she said. "As long as polocrosse is played on this field, as long as Minty's in good health, as long as I have hands to hold stick and reins, you haven't a hope."

"You always put up a good fight," he agreed. "Such skillful resistance when a lesser player would fold."

"I enjoy our battles. I plan to always come out on top."

He moved closer, into her space, and dipped his head toward her ear. Hot breath puffed on her neck. "Do you like being on top, Mel? I'd let you, y'know. You could be on top and ride me until we were both spent."

Her eyes closed momentarily in delight. It was so easy to bait him, so easy to taunt and flirt and ensnare him with double entendre until he had to walk away, hobbled by his own hard-on. She'd seen it before, a huge ridge filling his jeans.

"How presumptuous of you to assume you'll ever get to see me naked."

He chortled and instantly she realized her mistake.

"Who said anything about naked? I'm talking about polo-crosse. But if you want naked, you only have to ask."

"I've never thought of you naked," she lied. "As for polo-crosse, we'll never know who'll come out on top if we go one to one, so long as we both play attack."

In polocrosse, each chukka was played by three players:

attack, center and defense. The attack and the opposing defense were the only players allowed in the goal-scoring area, as they jostled for the upper hand, and a chance to snare the ball and shoot for goal or to flick it away to safety.

He put some distance between them, enough that she could see the glitter in his blue eyes. "Which is why I'm playing defense this game. I'll be playing opposite you."

Her eyes widened in anticipation. Now this could be interesting. Jack pushing close, leaning in to snare an errant ball. The shoving, the aggression, the sweat. The adrenaline, the arousal. It was all there in a good game of polocrosse, where an eight-minute chukka could feel like forever.

"Bring your best game," she said, and resumed her work with the dandy brush.

"I will. Want to make this extra interesting? Put some stakes on the outcome?"

"Sure. If I score more than ten goals, it's your shout in the bar. The entire bar."

"I was thinking higher than that." His voice tickled down her spine, low, quiet. Dangerous. "Cowboy downtime."

Cowboy downtime. Apart from polocrosse, there were few distractions in outback Queensland. Cards. Beer. Sleep. But traditional cowboy downtime usually involved the three *F*s: flirting, fighting, fucking. Mel had no doubt as to what Jack had in mind.

"Poker?" she stalled, as her mind raced to come up with an answer. "The only time we played, I left you in your jocks." A sight she had never forgotten. Jack's hard chest, golden and hairless, muscled legs, and bright blue underpants stretched tight over his erection.

"I wasn't thinking of cards."

A hundred blowflies buzzed in her stomach. Here it was:

the proposition she'd been angling for, for weeks now. Was she ready to pay up?

Hell, yeah.

She dropped the brush at Minty's feet, and paced forward, into his space. Grasping his shirt collar she pulled his head down to hers and slanted her mouth firmly over his. Her tongue pushed between his lips for a brief moment, tasting, dancing around his tongue before retreating. Her lips tingled and the taste of him was so overwhelming that it was a moment before she could catch breath enough to form words.

"Then I guess it's fucking." She licked her lips, cocked her head and gave him a hard, level stare. "If I score ten goals, you're mine tonight to do whatever I want with. Less than that, I'm yours. Deal?"

His hand curved possessively around her butt as he pulled her toward him. "Deal. Better buy a sheepskin for your saddle, Mel, 'cause you'll be sitting tender for a week."

"Better wear old clothes and bring your mop and bucket," she retorted. "I've got a very dirty house."

His chuckle drifted back to her as he sauntered off, treating her to the sight of his backside in those tight, tight denims.

The game started at two. Time enough for Mel to gulp a coffee and force down a sausage from the Lions Club barbeque. Jack was bigger than her, as was his mount, but size wasn't everything—at least not in polocrosse, she acknowledged with an inner chortle. Ten goals was high, but certainly not impossible; she'd scored more than that in the past—but Jack was an unknown quantity playing defense. She finished tacking up Minty with the low-pommeled English saddle and protective boots, mounted and went to join her teammates.

Jack's team was warming up on the far side of the field, tossing the ball back and forth. Clouds of red dust churned by the horses' galloping feet hung over the field, but she could still make out Jack, sitting easily on his chestnut mare, shifting his weight as the mare twisted and turned around the field.

Anticipation tingled low in her belly. Regardless of the outcome of the game, tonight would bring an explosive resolution to the long-simmering flirtation between her and Jack. She'd known for a long time they'd end up in bed, with nothing but skin between them. Their flirtation had been drawing closer to the pinnacle, the point where one of them had to give and make the first move. Anticipation prolonged the pleasure, but it was time for the conclusion.

The first chukka was slow. Players alternated chukkas, and as their best attack, Mel played the second, fourth and sixth chukkas. Dan, who played attack in the other section, did well, and at the end of the chukka their team, the Blue Flyers, had a three-to-one lead. But only her goals counted toward their bet.

She knew from the first line up it was going to be difficult. Jack stuck to her like a shadow, and his mare seemed welded to Minty's shoulder. Every twist and turn, every duck and weave, he was still there. She managed a break and streaked across the field, catching the ball in her net from their center. She was just outside the goal-scoring area, so she flicked it back and positioned herself inside, Jack's mare mere inches away. Dust hung over them in a pall from the horses' churning hooves. She dropped her weight to the right, but then pulled Minty hard to the left, and gained enough space to scoop the bounced ball flicked to her. Two fast strides and she shot for goal. The ball bulleted through the posts. One down.

Mel ignored Jack as they cantered back to the center. The game moved quickly. Two, three goals, then Jack's team scored one. One minute to go. She snared the ball, Minty wheeled, and Mel leaned forward urging her on. Jack was on her off side and his stick banged up against hers. Dislodged from the net, the ball spilled to the ground, but before Jack could scoop it up, Minty dropped her hindquarters and propped. Mel retrieved the ball and before Jack could stop his forward charge, she'd swung around and shot for goal. Four goals.

The chukka ended and she drew as deep a breath as she could over the pounding of her heart. Four out of ten. Not as many as she'd hoped. Jack urged his mare up alongside her.

"Worried, Mel?" His deep voice caressed her ears. "Wondering what you'll have to do tonight? How many times I'll take you?"

She peeled away from him, back to her teammates. "No," she shot back over her shoulder. "I'm going to win."

At the start of the sixth and final chukka, the game hung in the balance. Scores were tied. She took to the field to the cheers of her teammates and applause from the smattering of spectators lining the rail. For a moment she let herself soak up the atmosphere she loved: heat, dust and the dry and drooping landscape of outback Queensland. Horse sweat and leather.

Her inattention cost her, and her team was swiftly down two goals. "Get yer arse in gear, Mel!" yelled Dan from the railings, and she focused tight, caught the ball just inside the goal-scoring area. Two strides and she shot for goal. Seven down. Three to go.

The next couple of minutes passed in a blur. She scored again, and with a minute to go scored a lucky goal that just rolled through.

Her team was winning, but that wasn't what mattered to Mel. One more goal and a minute to do it. She gritted her teeth. Jack caught the ball, but she came up tight on his off shoulder and her stick crashed into his, freeing the ball. She scrambled for it, and scooped it up. Minty flattened her ears, her neck and shoulders wet with sweat, and galloped toward goal. Mel twisted, trying to get a clear shot, but Jack was with her, his mare matching every twist and turn with uncanny ability. There were seconds to go.

Mel raised the net, but Jack's mare dropped her shoulder and the horses crashed together. Off balance, Minty stumbled. Mel sat still, letting her regain her footing, but Jack was close, his thigh pushing into her own, their stirrup irons slamming together. Dust blinded her, as Jack's mare shoved Minty around, away from goal. Jack reached behind, trying to block her shot, but there was no need. His mare continued to shove, and Minty was forced off.

The game ended before the throw in could be taken. He came up alongside and grinned at her from under his helmet. "Good effort, darling. Nine goals. But not good enough. You're mine."

She shivered at his words, at the low, caressing tone, and at the way his eyes swept up her body to settle on her face. She pushed a sweaty tendril of her from her cheek. "A bet's a bet, Jack. I won't renege."

Turning, she headed for her float and set about unsaddling Minty and hosing her down to a chorus of shouted commiserations and good-natured insults from her teammates. When Minty was settled with a hay net, Mel went over to the make-shift counter that served as a bar on game days. She accepted a cold tinnie, but passed up on food; her churning stomach wouldn't allow her to eat. She knew the second Jack arrived to join the gathering. His broad-shouldered body drew her gaze as he took a beer and joined his teammates in a toast.

The beer lay sour in her stomach. Mel tipped it onto the brown grass and continued to circulate with an empty tinnie in her hand, pasting a fake smile on her face, wondering when Jack would come to claim her.

It was an hour later, when people were starting to drift away, back to stations and communities that were a couple of hours' drive away, that Jack approached her group, and his hand slid around Mel's waist.

"Time to go."

His arm lay hot around her waist, each fingerprint scorching her through her shirt. Sliding from his grasp, she said her fare-wells. Jack loped along at her side and the air between them crackled with tension.

"Where are we going?" she asked, more to break the silence than from a need to know. "I have to take Minty home first."

"My place. Minty can come along. There's a stall for her, or you can turn her out in the paddock with the others."

"You were that confident you'd win?" She knew she sounded petulant, but his casual assumption annoyed her.

They reached her float, where Minty lipped at fallen strands of hay.

Jack grabbed her arm and pushed her so they were hidden from passersby. The slats of the float pressed hard against her spine. Jack's hands palmed her hips, and he pushed his lower body against her.

His bulk loomed, but his touch was gentle as he tucked an errant curl of hair behind her ear. "Not confidence, Mel. Just cautious optimism. I was hoping."

His voice was low, smooth and almost tender, different from his normal bantering tone. He moved closer, and the sudden tightness in her chest made her breathe in shallow pants.

His lips moved closer, hovered over her own. "A little some-thing on account…"

And then he was kissing her, and she knew she was lost. His lips teased, tormented, fine lips, surprisingly soft, surprisingly gentle. Her pulse thundered in her ears and her breasts were suddenly uncomfortable, hard and aching, as they pushed against his chest. His kiss went on, past the point where she had breath of her own, past the point where she knew where she ended and he began. She was liquid heat and light, weak with wanting him.

He drew away slowly, returned to taste her once more and then withdrew again. When she opened her eyes his face filled her vision. He was smiling.

When she could trust her voice she said, "And that's just a kiss. What will happen when we fuck?"

He grinned in delight at her words. "I've been waiting for you to say that."

"What, 'fuck'?"

"No. For you to admit that we will."

She hooted. "I never thought you'd want to do otherwise with your bet. Are you going to tell me you want to spend the night knitting tea cozies?"

"You'll find out very soon what I want to do. But now we head home."

She followed him along dirt roads, through open range where cattle grazed, past dams ablaze with pink and gray galahs and flocks of sulphur-crested cockatoos. The sun hung low in the west, its clear light spilling over the flat landscape. They reached Bundawalla Station and Jack drew to a halt at the yards. The next twenty minutes were spent seeing to the horses.

Mel lingered, watching Minty roll in the dust. The heat of the day was fading to a comfortable warmth and the early stars were out. Cicadas filled the night with sound.

When she turned from the railing, Jack took her hand without a word, and led her toward the manager's house. The wide wraparound verandah of the old Queenslander was worn smooth, but swept clean. There was a couch on the side facing north, and a blind pulled half down to deflect the heat.

"Beer?"

She tilted her head to look up at him. "We both know what we're here for, and it isn't beer."

"Doesn't mean I'm without courtesy."

She turned to face him, and her fingers drifted to the waist of his dusty jeans. Her blood thrummed, pulsing in heated beats, energizing her. "I'm more interested in seeing what else you can do."

His thumb brushed briefly over her lips and then traced a lazy path down her neck to where her pulse skittered. "I don't think you'll have any complaints." His fingers pushed into the neck of her shirt, spreading over her collarbone, drumming lightly. "You're overdressed."

She took the hint, and her fingers moved to the buttons of her shirt.

But he grasped them, stilled the movement. "No, darling. This will be my pleasure." He slipped the buttons, so slowly, so carefully that his fingertips didn't graze her skin. When the shirt hung loose, he pushed it from her shoulders, and as his fingers trailed down her back she felt the catch of her bra loosen.

His eyes were dark and mysterious in the starlight. She toed off her boots, and then his fingers were at the waist of her jeans, unsnapping, unzipping, pushing them down over her hips with her panties. The dreamy lethargy of earlier was gone, and she tore at his clothes, fired up with lust and the need to feel him. The drumming in her head was a heated urgency, it pounded like the blood in her veins, it burned like the feel of his fingertips on her skin.

She bent and kicked her jeans away, impatient as they tangled and bunched. Jack threw his shirt down and discarded his own clothes, so that they lay in a tangled heap on the timber. "Can't wait, Mel, not anymore."

"Then don't," she replied, and pressed her naked body against his, skin to skin for the first time, chest to breast, thigh to thigh, his cock rising hard and proud between them.

He twitched at something hanging on the back of the couch. A sleeping bag, she realized, as he broke away from her to throw it to the floor, spreading it over their clothes. He drew her down, down to the soft cotton on sun-warmed timber, and his mouth was on hers and his body over hers.

She thrilled with the feel of him, with the urgency of it all, and the overwhelming need to feel him inside her. His cock bumped her thigh, and she raised her legs, cradled him with her hips, urging him on.

"Can't wait," he gasped again. "Foreplay—"

"We've been foreplaying all day," she said. "I want you now." Impatience surged within her. She didn't want subtle or delicate, or long and slow; she wanted fast and hard; she wanted to be filled, to know his solidity within her. She wanted to be fucked.

He changed the angle of his body, and his cock nudged her folds. She canted her hips toward him and he slid inside with one smooth movement. Mel arched her back, clenched down. The feeling of fullness, the fat slide of him inside was enough to send frissons of pleasure deep into her belly.

She closed her eyes, concentrating on the sensation as he started to advance and retreat. His hips were solid between her thighs. She dug her fingers into his buttocks, urging him on. His face pressed against the crook of her neck, his breath hot and urgent on her skin. She wanted his finger on her clit because it wasn't enough with him inside her. And then he raised up on his hands, and suddenly it was enough, and he was hot and hard, moving hard and fast, and spirals of light danced behind her closed eyelids.

"Mel," he said, his voice hoarse with effort, "look at me darling. I want you to know who's inside you."

She opened her eyes, and his face filled her vision. He was holding back, she realized, waiting for her. Tenderness overwhelmed her, and she curled a palm around his cheek. "I know who I'm fucking," she said. "You, Jack. Only you." And then the spasms started deep in her belly, long drawn-out waves of pleasure that rolled through her like the tide, advancing and retreating.

As her orgasm subsided she found he was coming too in deep thrusts and a spreading liquid heat. He rolled over, taking her with him, so that she straddled his prone body. His cock softened but remained tucked inside. His hips undulated and aftershocks of pleasure coursed through her.

Jack's hand drew idle patterns on her thigh. "We're not done yet."

"Confident?" she teased. "You don't need recovery time?"

"I do," he said, and his hand moved to cover her mound. "But you don't." His thumb found her nub and rubbed it softly. "I'm going to stroke you…" His thumb passed once more over her clit. " And suck you here—" Raising up, his mouth opened over one nipple. "And here." The other nipple. "Then you're going to suck my cock until I'm hard, and I'll taste that pussy of yours." His hips pushed up into her again. "By then, we might be ready for the second chukka."

She gazed down at him, her fingers mapping the way forward on his smooth chest. "Better get started then."

In answer, he lifted her away from his body and laid her back on the sleeping bag. The ceiling fan stirring the warm air before it was blocked by Jack's big body.

He kissed her neck, the hollow of her throat where a pulse beat furiously, and moved down. His tongue dragged moist pathways down her breasts, and when he took a nipple in his mouth a shaft of scarlet pleasure made her cry out.

"Touch me," Jack commanded.

And she complied, tracing the sun-bronzed skin of his forearms, down along his chest to where his copper nipples jutted, down farther to where his cock rose from its nest of hair. Not hard yet, but tumescent. She palmed the shaft, ran fingers over the head, pushing his foreskin down and up. His cock twitched, lengthened and hardened.

Jack moved farther down, and her fingers fell away from his cock as he moved between her legs. A brief pain bloomed as he bit lightly on her inner thigh. Then his face was between her legs, his tongue on her clit, and the world went hazy and faint, and there were stars behind her eyelids as well as in the sky.

Jack turned, straddling her body so that his cock hung heavy, bumping her lips with mute appeal.

Mel licked the tip, tasting herself and his own musky scent.

His tongue flickered on her clit, pushing her up to her peak, and she gave herself over to the sensation, coming hard against his face.

Eager to repay, she sucked him in, using lips and tongue until her nose rested in his sweat-damp hairs. His balls tightened hard against his body, and then he lifted her and sat her over his hips.

"You wanted to ride me," he whispered.

She raised up on strong thighs, lowered onto his cock, feeling once again the thick slide of him inside her. Strange how he was already familiar, as if he was destined to be her lover. Mel rode him hard, a slide and a slam and a crash of motion, a frenzied coupling that was all too short as he spurted inside her once again.

She rested her hands on his chest as her breathing slowed to normal. "Are you always like that?"

He grinned, proud of his prowess. "Only with you. Why did we wait so long to do this?"

She shrugged. "You won the bet, but I'm doing well out of this."

His hand cupped her cheek and the tenderness in his touch made her catch her breath. "It was always about you, Mel. The bet was an excuse. I want you to come back to me after tonight."

She couldn't answer him in words, but covered his hand with her own, rocking into his palm.

He scooted out from underneath her and rose to his feet, extending a hand. Entwining his fingers with hers, unselfconscious in his nakedness, he led her to the verandah railing. Together they stared out at the soft night.

"I might not have been as easy on you if I'd won."

His rich chuckle stirred her hair. "You'd be hard on me, would you? I think I can handle that."

"Don't be too sure. If I score ten goals next game—"

He pulled her close. "It's a bet."

COMING HOME

Megan Mitcham

G ravel crunched under the massive pickup's tires as it left smooth pavement behind. Barrett's chest constricted in response. Breathing became hard. Hell, the rebellion his insides pitched was close kin to a panic attack, but cowboys, whole or broke down, didn't have such weak-kneed reactions. The panorama before him of vast rolling hills, green, cow-sprinkled grass and wide-open sky was home. Six years away hadn't dimmed its beauty or his affection. Barrett rolled his shoulders and shrugged off the vibe. Nothin' to get riled about.

Barrett crested the first hill and knew he had every right to feel screwed up inside. Two sorrel mares, one a good hand taller and three hundred pounds stouter than the other, blocked the gravel driveway. A petite woman with long, strawberry, wind-whipped hair, wearing boots and chaps, sat astride the smaller horse. Her elegant jaw was set in a familiar expression of stubborn rage.

"Holy fuck!" The words left his mouth in a drawled whisper.

He halted the pickup and confronted her fierce gaze with his own. The air between them grew thick with tension like an ol' western draw. Finally, she swirled a finger in the air, signaling him to roll down the window. Being a gentleman, he obliged.

She planted a delicate hand on her hip. "You didn't really think you were gonna sneak back home while everybody's gone to auction, did you?"

The air blew crisp and clean in his face as he draped one arm on the door. "Yeah, I's countin' on it actually."

"Anyone you lookin' to avoid?" she asked, straightening, her silky pink lips tightening.

That face, part angel, part nymph, never ceased to amaze him. Neither did the rest of her. His eyes dropped to her bite-sized breasts and his cock saluted, thickening in his jeans. "Naw." His lips parted again, but the words died in an expelled breath. Too soon for all that.

Pale lids narrowed around flame-green eyes. Her nose twitched, drawing his attention to the spray of freckles that ran across its ridge and over delightful apple cheeks. Then her lips moved. "A wise man would, but since you aren't—lookin' to avoid anyone, that is—git your tush out of that truck before my panties melt off."

Damn, if his chest didn't tighten again. He pounded his fist against the sensation, adjusted his hat, and leaned closer to the fiery woman. "Excuse me?"

"That is the point of that sexy machine, to make women drop their drawers?"

The laugh came from deep inside, from a place so hidden light hadn't touched it in years. "Sassy Britches, it's been a while. You've changed, and then you haven't."

"Barrett Whitman, if you wanna make it home, you won't call me that again. I don't care if you are 'The Bear,' four-yearreignin' National Rodeo Champion. Get your ass out the truck and on this horse."

"Scarlett, you keep talkin' like that, and I'll be forced to tell your daddy. I'd hate for him to have to paddle your sweet bottom."

She gave a girlie, "Huh!" and then wiggled narrow hips as she spoke. "If you'd been around, you'd know my daddy's retired back home to Texas and your parents saw fit to put me in charge of the ranch. Now, scoot. Daylight's wastin', and we got some ground to cover."

Dust puffed up around his boots as they hit the ground. Scarlett tried her best to ignore the grimace that briefly tightened his face. Instead, she reveled in the familiar mix of pleasure and pain the sight of him wrought. She held her mouth slack and breathed slowly, fighting the excitement and urge to pounce. With new eyes and old love, she watched Barrett hobble toward the perfect example of equine physique.

His sharp, brilliant-blue gaze examined the big mare. After a moment, he leaned wide shoulders closer.

The mare rewarded his interest with a sniff of his starched white button-down.

One side of his perfect mouth curved as he caressed her flaxen mane.

Scarlett's eyes went wide, tracking his touch and wishing like the devil his thick calloused fingers were on her neck, face, back, legs. Anywhere, as long as his skin met hers. Warmth rushed to her jean-covered crotch, dampening the fabric, the longing an exquisite agony. It prickled her spine, extinguished the erotic fire in her pants, and reignited her anger.

Her voice held no hint of the weakness she felt inside. "Hop on."

His dark brow shot up, and his hand dropped from the mare's neck like he'd been shot. For a long moment their gazes held. In those brief seconds, Scarlett was alive, electrified by the connection so long ago abandoned.

Barrett hooked a thumb in his pocket. His already full lips pursed in a bewildered pout.

Scarlett swallowed hard, fighting the urge to taste them.

That bright-blue gaze left her face, surveyed his bum leg, then returned. "Maybe later."

"No. Now."

His voice rumbled. "Woman, I'm not some kid who fell off and busted his rear."

"No, you're not. You're a man who got busted by a two-ton beast. He stomped your leg, some ribs, and nearly ended your life. You're a man who longs for the life and abilities you had before Tulsa, and you're terrified of an uncertain future.

"So, you can lay up at the old homestead feeling sorry for yourself, instead of takin' hold of all the things you still have to live for, but you'll not be the man I used to know. If you're still Barrett Whitman, the charm-slingin', bull-crackin', bronco-bustin' cowboy in your heart, you rebuild one ride at a time."

Moments piled in silence. Scarlett watched the rise and fall of his sturdy chest, the clench and release of his square, stubble-covered jaw. Slowly, he shuffled toward the saddle. "I liked you better when you were a dumb kid."

"I liked you better then, too."

One hand gripped the horn and the other clutched the cantle. "Scarlett?"

Her heart bucked. "That's the first time you've ever said my name."

"No, it's not." A wicked grin flashed.

Scarlett felt it all the way to her toes and nearly stumbled over her own lips. "When did you ever say my name?"

The grin returned. "I'd make your pretty cheeks color, if I explained."

Idiot. Scarlett could kick her own chap-bare ass, walking into Bear's charm trap so easily. Growing up, she'd witnessed him finesse the britches off many a sweetheart. Most times, he didn't have to try. He'd tilt his hat, smile and they'd turn into bitches in heat, moaning and carrying on like he was some sex god.

She was the only one he wouldn't dally with, likely because they'd been raised side by side, and he thought of her as sister. She'd never know his reasoning. All she knew was the broken heart of a girl who'd asked the only boy she'd ever loved to kiss her like he'd kissed his many girlfriends. He'd turned her down and left for the rodeo circuit two months later.

His flat voice snapped her to the present. "Anyway, Scarlett. If I hit the dirt…"

For the first time she saw vulnerability in his features. The fissure in her heart grew. Uncertainty never had a home in Barrett, the man who chose the wildest horses and craziest bulls to pit his skills against. To save his pride she said, "I'll be sure to laugh."

His lips curved wide in the dearest of smiles. "Bet you would."

Her hand shot out. "Wait."

"What now?" he asked before settling both hands on his hips.

She waived her reins at him. "Take off your shirt."

"You want me naked, all you have to do is say the words."

She narrowed her gaze. "I don't suppose you'd want to get that nice shirt dirty—you know, if you hit the ground and all—but thanks for the advice. Now take it off and up you go," she said, prodding him on with a flick of her wrist.

"Impatient woman."

"I've been more than patient with you," she murmured. And wasn't that the truth. "Too damn patient."

Barrett huffed and went to work on his buttons. He unfastened each one with deliberate care, revealing a thin white undershirt as he went. It wasn't skin, but the material molded to his broad chest.

The teasing manner in which he undressed turned the warm breeze into stifling air. A bead of sweat plunged between Scarlett's breasts, and she willed the torture to end.

At last the fasteners were free, and Barrett licked his lips. He slid the material off, exposing arms thickly corded with muscle, and then jammed the shirt into the saddlebag.

Damn the man to hell and back. She watched in locked awe, unable to look away as he gripped the saddle, sprung on his good leg and hoisted his large frame onto the saddle. His muscles bunched, showing the outline of a defined six-pack. A tiny bead of sweat rolled down his cheek and along the edge of his sumptuous bottom lip. But none of that held her singular concentration like the massive bulge in his pants.

Barrett couldn't do a damn thing about the uncomfortable swell of wood he sported. At least seventy ways to relieve the pressure stampeded through his mind, and they all included Scarlett's body in one compromising position or another. But that would be like going from zero to forty on the back of a wild mustang. Still, he couldn't lasso the words that flew out of his mouth. "Well, you gonna stare at my dick all day or toss me the reins?"

Scarlett's cheeks flushed as red as the old barn, but she smiled. Thin lips outlined a nice set of pearlies, even if she did have one slightly kicked-out canine. Her eyes beckoned him. This close, the warmth of that smile branded his heart.

She stood in the saddle, driving her heal into the stirrup, and shortened the gap between them. "Kiss me, Barrett."

His heart did the electric slide right out of his chest. The desire to yank her into his lap and obey made his palms sweat. But there was so much between them. History. Friendship. Yearning. The thought of screwing things up with Scarlett, of never eliciting that honeyed smile from her again, flash-froze him to the cowhide under his rear.

A moment later she stiffened and sank into her seat. Without a word she pitched the leathers to him. The other hand turned her horse toward the grass-covered hill. The firm heel of her boot compelled the mare forward like a racer out of the gate. And he was left in her dust.

She fled in self-preservation. Her body ached for him. She had to get away or risk throwing herself at his feet more than she already had. He hadn't said no, but something had widened his eyes. Fear. Shock. Who knew? But she was finished bowing to the mighty bull rider.

Easier said than done. Visions of her at his feet invaded her mind. Scarlett on her knees before him, baring his thick cock, inviting it into her eager mouth. Saliva pooled on Scarlett's tongue, and with all her virgin heart, she wished Barrett's thick juices were sliding down her throat.

She was so enraptured in the dream, she choked on reality.

Barrett's hand shot out and grabbed her horse's bridle.

She tried slapping him away while they barreled up a steep hill. But a deep, "Whoa," ushered the animal to a stop at the crest. They halted on their mounts, knees touching.

Barrett glared. "Jesus, Scarlett, are you tryin' to kill yourself?"

"Me?" The shrill word echoed into the small valley below.

"I'm not the one who ran off to dance with two-horned devils every night. I mean...shit, Barrett. You didn't want to kiss me, didn't like me—*okay*—but you didn't have to leave."

"Yeah, I did."

Her next word came in a sob. "Why?"

Again, his jaw clenched. In a graceless move, he bailed off the saddle and strode, as much as his limp would allow, around the horses, stopping when his chest met her thigh.

When he pulled her off her horse, Scarlett went willingly.

His body pinned her against the warm animal. On either side he draped an arm so she couldn't escape. "I loved you, Scarlett."

"Like a brother loves his sister?" she asked, jaw raised in defiance.

He brushed a tear from her cheek. "Like a husband loves his wife," he whispered. His thumb moved from her cheek down the length of her jaw to graze her lips parted in shock. "I remember the day you and your daddy moved into the ranch master's house. Your mom had just passed, and you were the meanest kid I'd ever met, back-talkin' the adults and scarin' away kids twice your age. You didn't scare me. I called you Sassy Britches and promised to protect you always.

"I taught you to ride any strong-willed horse and cuss before kindergarten. In grade school, I showed you how to rope, cut cattle and run the fastest set of barrels this side of Colorado. During middle school, I coached you on throwin' a decent punch to keep the boys in line."

His breath left in a slow gust. "Then high school rolled around. Everything changed so fast. Your body blossomed into the loveliest creation on this damn earth. I had trouble enough keepin' myself in check. When you asked me to kiss you, I knew if I started I wouldn't stop. My lips craved to taste every part of you. My hands itched to touch your soft skin. You were a kid, becomin' a woman, but still so pure. I was seasoned, to put it kindly, already a man, and I'd promised to protect you. As it turned out, I was the one you needed protecting from."

When she opened her mouth to speak, he pressed a finger against her lips. "Leavin' home was hard, but nothin' compared to not seein' your honest smile every day, hearin' your excitement or sass-mouthed anger. I left to protect you and make somethin' out of myself so you'd be proud to call me yours."

Scarlett bit back tears that threatened to spill. She ran two hands across Barrett's work-hardened abdomen up to his chest. With all the force in her small body, she shoved against him. "Sure as shit took you long enough," she growled.

Being over a foot taller and almost a hundred pounds heavier, he didn't budge from her assault. In fact, he smiled and opened his mouth to speak.

But she beat him to it by blurting, "I'm gettin' married in June."

Barrett's smile fell, his face ashen, and he stepped back. His thumbs found his pockets, and he glared at his boots. "Any talkin' you out of it?" he asked, his voice rasping.

"No. I'm in love."

He turned a half step away from her and looked out at the horizon. She followed his line of sight. From up there the river looked like a blue snake winding its way over the land. Clouds were close enough to touch. Air was clean and peppered with the scent of wild spring blooms. The wide expanse of green and blue made their drama feel closer, more intimate, real.

"He's a lucky man." Laughter brought his gaze up fast.

"He sure is. Lucky I don't kill him for goin' off and leavin' me heartbroken and wonderin' what I'd done wrong for six long years."

"What are you sayin', Scarlett?" he asked, with a hint of desperation.

"I'm say you're marryin' me in June, and there's not a thing you can do to change it."

If the impact of his chest barreling into hers wasn't enough to knock the wind out of her, his crushing hug was. One second her feet touched the ground, the next she was swept up in Barrett's embrace. His lips dappled kisses across her brow, down the bridge of her nose, across each cheek and the line of her jaw. When he reached her neck, he swept thick locks of her red hair over her shoulder. The sensitive skin tingled as his kiss grew more compelling. The warmth of his tongue caressed her skin, leaving slick trails that cooled in the breeze. Teeth nipped at her collarbone.

Desperate for his mouth on hers, she grabbed his face.

Finally, his soft ample lips collided with her own. His hands knotted in her hair as he maneuvered her head, gaining better access to her thirsty mouth. Their tongues tangled and tasted.

Need, carnal and urgent, flared inside Scarlett's body. She lassoed chap-covered legs around Barrett's waist, pulling him tight against her core.

Grabbing two handfuls of her ass, Barrett adjusted her across the hard ridge of his penis.

A moan poured from her lips into his mouth as he rocked slowly and ground their bodies together. Friction burned. Jeans chafed. Her clit spasmed, and she bucked wildly with a climax. Scarlett's back bowed, then contracted in rapid succession, milking the sensation. Her last fit tumbled them over onto the knee-high grass.

Barrett rolled on top and kissed a trail down her body, unfastening buttons, unclasping buckles and freeing zippers as he went. "Christ, Scarlett. Next time don't wear so many clothes."

Still panting and enjoying aftershocks of her first orgasm with another human being, Scarlett nodded in agreement.

After freeing every inch of her body from the confines of denim, cotton and leather, Barrett sat back on his heels. His studied her from head to toe without a word or touch, and then smiled.

The adoring gesture washed Scarlett in confidence. She sat and kissed him firmly. Her hands gasped the fabric of his shirt and peeled the thing off his torso. He shucked his pants and boots in record time, and Scarlett sat back to examine her man.

She had to bite her lip to quiet the *Wow!* threatening to escape. He was like nothing she'd ever seen before. Sculpted as a man should be. The lines of his body highlighted in lean muscle. His skin bronzed from long days working in the sun.

His cock jutted out from a tuft of dark hair. It bobbed with his pulse and seemed to grow with each passing beat. Tentatively, Scarlett reached for the rod of silky flesh.

Barrett pushed her back onto the ground. "First things first, Sassy. We'll do show-and-tell later." He covered her, his large body blocking the mid-morning's light.

By instinct, she spread her legs wide ready to receive him.

One strong arm braced her against his chest. The other propped his large body above her. Contact began with a soft rock of his hips. His cock grazed her slick folds.

Scarlett arched her body, prolonging the touch. The hair on his chest abraded her nipples, and suddenly it wasn't enough. She angled her hips and his fat tip found home, sinking an inch or two. Against his shoulder she muffled a gasp. Delight warred with agony.

He pulled out and she ached for more. His tip entered and withdrew time and again until Scarlett dug her heels into his buttocks and drew him deeper. She readied herself for more, bending and opening for him, but Barrett stilled.

Breathing labored between them for a moment. Then with careful precision, Barrett asked quietly, "Scarlett, baby, are you a virgin?"

A small chuckle escaped her throat. "Been waitin' to give it to you since I knew what it was, and if you don't take it already, I'm headin' to town and givin' it to the first man I see."

In response, Barrett thrust deeper with each rock of his hips, capturing what she offered.

A tear of relief rolled down her cheek as she rocked with him. Scarlett rolled her hips, working the length of his shaft with her tight pussy. Deep inside she felt the pinch of his dick stretching her tight passage, the massage of its girth rubbing her slippery walls. Outside, her clit beat against his pelvis.

The rhythm increased to a frantic pace.

Barrett bit her earlobe and drawled, "Come for me, baby."

The demand lit an explosive orgasm. Her insides reverberated from the power of it. Scarlett squeezed her eyelids shut in rapture while he pounded deeper, driving her into the earth until he groaned.

Scarlett's eyes flew open when Barrett pulled out of her body. She marveled as he gripped the column of his dick firmly in his fist, it's bulbous head exposed.

Barrett's chin lifted toward the sky. His breath suspended. The wide tip of his penis turned red, then purple and seemed to grow before jets of white erupted from it, sprinkling her belly.

Barrett fell to the grass, threw an arm over Scarlett and pulled her close. In between deep breaths he said, "Condoms. We need condoms. Can't get you pregnant...yet."

"Well," Scarlett said, "I don't have any condoms."

He propped on his elbow and began cleaning her off with his discarded shirt. "Didn't expect you would. I have some in my truck."

"Why didn't you say so?" Scarlett asked, while she shoved his hand away and jumped to her feet. Standing naked on the hillside, she rifled through their strewn clothes.

"Sass, what are you doin'?"

"I'm goin' to the truck."

She pulled jeans over her bare bottom and winked at Barrett. "Wanna race?"

HER CAPTURED
COWBOY

Layla Chase

Overhead, thick, puffy clouds hung low in the eastern sky. The midday sun beat on Bo Hadrian as his horse, Midnight, picked out the easiest trail down the Sangre de Cristo Mountains. Air as heated as if he stood beside a blacksmith's forge attacked his nose. This part of Colorado Territory was best suited for lizards, tarantulas and snakes—a place where an ex-bounty hunter like him felt right at home.

Stones skittered downhill, snapping and popping off boulders, and Midnight stumbled, his front hooves slipping several feet down the incline.

"Easy." Bo tightened his grip on the reins and leaned his hips against the cantle. His gaze scanned the rocky landscape for the movement of any stray cattle. Three hours since breaking off from the main herd, and he hadn't spotted a single animal to hustle back to the Triple R Ranch.

Midnight lifted his nose and snorted with a shake of his head.

The rush of water running over rocks reached him before he smelled the clean, fresh scent. Ah, a soaking would feel great right about now. Giving Midnight his head, Bo glanced around the scraggly pines and aspens, ever alert to shadows under and behind boulders.

Murmurs and guffaws sounded from behind the cluster of madrone bushes. "Oo-wee, looky that. See them big, round titties."

Damnation. Bo's body tensed, and he kneed Midnight's shoulders, easing the animal along the path.

"And that coppery thatch."

Rounding the last bushes, Bo spotted the broad backsides of a couple of pairs of ragged overalls. He leaned a forearm on the saddle horn and rested his hand on the butt of his holstered revolver...and waited. Men could be such jackasses over a bit of bared female flesh. No doubt liquor was involved.

He cleared his throat and watched both men jerk and slowly straighten. Thumbing back his hat, he squinted his eyes into narrow slits and gave them the glare that had made plenty of criminals pause.

"We're just leaving." Looking everywhere but at the man on the horse, the men shoved at each other. They turned and ran in the opposite direction, crashing through bushes.

Sweat trickled along his temples and he lifted his hat, scrubbing his forearm over his damp forehead. The sound of splashing reached his ears, and he craned his neck. Through the green foliage, he spotted movement near the waterfall—long slender limbs and creamy white skin. An immediate jolt of lust tightened his groin. "Hey, lady in the falls."

A flash of wavy red hair and rounded ass disappeared beneath the water. She surfaced near a rock and grabbed a long hunting knife, breathing hard. "Who's there?"

Her voice was raspy and low, deepening his attraction. "Your audience is gone."

"My audience? I don't know your voice, stranger. Show yourself."

Bo urged Midnight closer to the water's edge and tipped a forefinger to the edge of his hat. "Bo Hadrian, ma'am."

Her body bobbed an inch lower in the water, her gaze shifting to the surrounding bushes. While she studied him, she kept an arm moving to disrupt the pool's water.

With determination, he forced his gaze above the water's depth, even though every male cell in his body screamed for another look at her creamy skin. "I'm alone, ma'am."

"Don't move closer. And don't even think about stealing my clothes." The woman shifted a couple of feet to the right. As she jerked her head around to scan the perimeter of the pool, she lifted the knife and jabbed the wide blade in his direction.

Tightening his knees, he urged the horse forward, all the while holding up his hands, palms out. "Like I said, I'm alone, ma'am."

Midnight bent his head and slurped at the water.

"Don't call me that." Her chin jerked upward, and she flipped wet strands of hair over a rounded shoulder. "I stopped being a lady the summer I was twelve."

The hollow tone of her voice stabbed him in the chest. What could have happened to cause that? "Those scalawags won't be back."

"I can take care of myself." Her light blue eyes narrowed, and she jutted out her chin.

"I see that." Her vigilance showed him she'd been alone for a while. Feistiness in a woman was sexy as hell. He couldn't stop his lips from spreading into a smile. "Just ridding the area of vermin before I take a swim."

"Don't much matter. Giving those fools a peek now and then is the price I pay to live near town." She rested the knife on the top of a boulder, sunlight glinting along its honed blade.

What the hell kind of arrangement was that? The need to defend overtook him, and he swung from the saddle, tossing the reins onto a nearby bush. "That water sure looks good. You about finished here?" With quick jerks, he loosened the knot in the kerchief from around his neck and swabbed it across his throat.

"Sure, why not?" The woman spun and stroked across the pool.

Thick welts crisscrossed her back, and Bo winced at the sight of her severe punishment, his gut shriveling into a knot. He'd seen marks like that before on captives of Indian tribes.

"I'm getting my clothes. Turn around."

Grinning, Bo pulled out the tails of his shirt and turned his back to the pool. That swim was gonna feel real good. Washing off the trail dust was just what he needed.

A rock bounced into the water with a plop. "The pool is yours."

"Thank you, ma'am." Hands on his belt buckle, he pivoted on his boot heel and spotted her at the head of the trail, clad in a fringed buckskin Indian dress, her feet encased in moccasins. Her pale skin and wavy red hair contrasted with the clothing, but the brandished knife looked like it fit. "Might I know your name?"

"Meghan Hegarty." A shoulder lifted in a shrug. "I'm the local healer." With a smooth move, she sheathed the knife into the scabbard hanging at her waist and walked out of sight.

For several seconds, he stood in place, his thoughts on the puzzle the strange woman presented. Then he shucked his clothes, piled them on his saddle, and waded into the pool until he could duck beneath the surface, letting the cool water sluice the grit from his body. Ah, so refreshing. Five strokes took him across the pool, and he tucked to turn in the opposite direction and surfaced, blinking water away from his eyes.

A double-action metallic ratchet filled the air.

Bo jerked his head to the edge of the pool where Midnight waited. *Aw, hell.* His chest pinched.

Beside the horse stood Meghan, his rifle leveled at her hip. "That's right, swim over here."

"What are you doing?"

"Climb out and get on your clothes. We're going for a ride."

He glanced around, searching for a way out of this mess. "I've got three bucks in my saddlebags. Sorry, but payday's not for another two weeks." As he walked forward, the water dipped lower along his muscled frame. Two final strides brought him to the damp dirt at the edge of the pool. Water ran off his body in rivulets and pooled at his feet. He jammed his hands on his hips.

Meghan's gaze dropped to his waist, and her eyes widened, the gun wavering a few inches lower. She bit her lower lip and then a slow smile grew.

His traitorous body reacted to her response, and his cock lengthened along his thigh. "Toss me my clothes."

Keeping her gaze locked on him, she raised her left hand to the saddle, grabbed his jeans, and tossed them his way.

Bo caught the warmed denim and shoved his feet into the pant legs. How had he let a female get the drop on him? In ten years of bounty hunting, that had only occurred once. That one incident prompted his decision to leave the job of searching for outlaws to younger gun hands. Much safer to hunt down stray cattle.

Until now.

"My shirt?" When he turned, Meghan had stepped back several feet.

"Won't need it. Grab your boots and let's get going." She waved the rifle toward Midnight with a jerk.

He eyed the strap of his holster around the saddle horn. Maybe he could get his pistol while stepping into his boots. Or he could slip a hand into the saddlebag where he kept his spare revolver. At Midnight's side, he leaned a shoulder against the horse's withers as he brushed pebbles off the bottom of his foot. But the angle was wrong—she'd see any attempt to reach a weapon. Pissed at being at her mercy, he stomped into his boots and reached for his shirt still lying across the saddle.

Pain exploded in the back of his head and his vision went black.

Meghan struggled, her legs quivering with the effort to push the cowboy onto her mattress. Once she'd shouldered him up to sprawl belly-down over the saddle, she figured the toughest hurdle was crossed. But the well-muscled, dark-eyed man was heavier than she'd thought. She blew out a breath and yanked on the blanket she'd used to drag him into her cabin, releasing one edge to roll him onto the ticking.

Her first sight of this handsome man at the waterfall sparked a plan. A woman who'd been held captive for a dozen years by Indians didn't stand a chance at receiving a second look by a decent man. But this cowboy had shooed off those fools who wouldn't know how to do anything but ogle her flesh. He'd honored her privacy and treated her with respect. He'd proven himself worthy.

If she wasn't so hellfire bent on having a man between her thighs, she might have felt a twinge of guilt about bashing him over the head. With quick moves, she stripped him of his boots and jeans and used rawhide thongs to tie his hands and feet to the bedposts. Only a few moments were spent on securing his horse in her lean-to outside, setting out a pan of grain and a bucket of water.

Then she returned to the cabin to shed her dress and rub mint leaves over her body. Not like the French perfume her mama had used, but Meghan had adopted many of the Indian ways. A fact that probably kept her an outsider, even on this Colorado frontier.

Two years had passed since an Army attack on Chief Rising Cloud's tribe of Cheyenne released her from her capture. The soldiers had dumped her in the closest settlement of Ouray. Barely remembering how to speak English, she'd been at a disadvantage from the outset. Kindly church folks provided shelter and meals and refreshed her language skills. But after a few months, she'd relocated to an abandoned miner's cabin to escape the distrust in the eyes of the townspeople, especially the women.

Standing at the foot of the bed, she gazed upon the bulges and planes of Bo's body. Dark hair contrasted with the skin of his calves and thighs—so different from the bare skin of the Indian brave, Bright Eagle, who'd claimed her as a wife. Curly hair on his groin cushioned the cock that lay broad and thick on his left thigh. As she watched, the shaft lengthened and rose away from his body. Amazing, even in his sleep.

Her gaze snapped up to his face. His dark eyes glared from under scowling eyebrows.

"What are you doing?"

His raspy growl sent a shiver up her spine, and her nipples tightened into beads. Knowing he couldn't fight his response to her nakedness, she felt emboldened. "Taking what I need."

To gain the most pleasure from an experience that may have to last her a long time, she started a slow caress of her own body. Trailing one hand over her belly and hips, she used the other to cup and mold her aching breasts. A sigh released through her lips, and she slid around to the far side of the bed.

"This is wrong." The muscles in his arms bunched as he struggled against the restraints.

His words halted her movement, and she rested one knee on the bed frame. Wrong? This simple act could not compare. "Wrong was my kidnapping when I was a child. Wrong was stealing my innocence when I should have been stitching my first sampler. Wrong was taking away my—" Tears burned the backs of her eyes, and she sucked in a breath to combat the loss that had hardened a piece of her heart.

Forcing a smile, she waved a hand at his erection that now stood stiff like the pole of a tepee. "Your interest is evident." She slid beside his body, reveling in his heat. Her hands moved over taut skin, feeling the coiled strength of muscles that performed hard work. Hours in the saddle made strong thighs and rock-hard calves.

"Can't help my natural reaction." His body tensed. "Don't do this."

For a moment, her hand rested on his abdomen, feeling the bugles and valleys between each muscle. "Why not? I've been a wife, and now I need a man." Her head shot up, and she glared into his eyes. All her adult life she watched as people took from her what they wanted, ignoring her wishes. For once, she wanted something, and she had worked to get him here. His words would not stop her.

He met her stare, his gaze narrowing a bit, but he remained mute. His whole body was as taut as a bowstring.

Meghan pushed herself to her knees and lifted her hands to

cup her breasts. "Do you not want to touch me? Am I not... fit?" She swallowed back the word "pretty" because that wasn't important. She was a woman who needed to be fucked and here was a fine specimen to do just that.

"Not like this."

What did this cowboy know? Closing her eyes, she caressed her body with long strokes to the rhythm of a remembered chant taught by a wise Indian woman who'd befriended her. The chant lifted Meghan away into a world where pain couldn't reach.

With gentle tugs, she plucked her nipples until they stood pert and pointy, the sensation zinging straight to her core. Her pussy clenched and dewy drops trickled along her nether lips. Without another thought, she straddled Bo's hips and centered her pussy over his cock, circling and lowering herself inch by inch onto the broad shaft. At first, his girth burned her channel, and she sucked in a breath until her body relaxed and accepted the invasion. Then pleasure overtook her senses as she rocked her body along his length. Too long had she gone without feeling filled, too long had her agile fingers provided her only release.

Bracing her hands on his stomach, she rode his cock hard, pumping her hips and hearing the slap of her asscheeks against his thighs. Her breasts swung and bounced with each thrust, keeping her nipples tight. Arousal tightened her clittie, and she angled her hips to grind that sensitive pearl against his crisp groin hairs. A move that had always achieved the desired result. But this time, her orgasm wouldn't explode. The arousal deep in her belly slowly unwound and dissipated.

What had just happened? A sense of deep shame constricted her chest. Breaths rasped through her lips, and tears clogged her throat.

When she was sure her expression was under control, she glanced at Bo's face. His jaw was clamped tight, and his cheeks were rigid as he stared to the side, out the window. An all-too-familiar posture—one she'd adopted many times at the beginning of her capture.

With a strangled sob, she stumbled off the bed, tossed a blanket over her shoulders, and dashed outside. Only then did she let the emotion wash through her and allow the tears to stream down her cheeks. Too many years of self-preservation had twisted her heart. Maybe she deserved to be on her own, maybe this place on the fringe of society was all she'd be allowed.

"Meghan, come back. Talk to me."

Bo's words held no rancor but just a hint of need. No man wanted to feel vulnerable, and hog-tied and naked was about as vulnerable as one could be.

Using the edge of the blanket to wipe her face, she heaved a sigh and stepped back into the cabin. She swapped the blanket for her dress, shoved her feet into her moccasins, making sure to slip a small knife inside her right boot. Then she stood several feet from the bed, head bowed. "I'm ready to free you, but only if you promise not to punish me."

"Meghan, look at me."

Shame and guilt filled her, and she wasn't brave enough to look again into his dark eyes. Gone would be the laughing expression she'd been drawn to at the pool. Instead, they'd be filled with retribution and blame, and that wasn't the way she wanted to remember her cowboy. She moved to the foot of the bed and loosened the knots in the thongs, keeping her gaze focused on her task. Next she untied his left hand, saving his strong hand for last, and shuffled back to the foot of the bed.

His hand dropped to the mattress with a thud and Bo let out a groan. "Damn, my arm's on fire."

Meghan moved to the right side and bent over to slip out her knife when a strong pull on the back of her dress toppled her onto the mattress. Right into an iron-hard embrace.

"If you won't look at me, maybe I can get you to listen."

As best she could, she struggled, trying to free her arms, but he was too strong. Her back was clamped tight to his chest, and she was trapped. Blood pounded in her ears, and her heart raced. When she kicked backward, he threw a leg over hers and tightened his thighs.

"Shh, relax. I won't hurt you, Meghan."

His warm breath moved the wavy hair that escaped her braid and tickled her earlobe. Even if for the wrong reasons, she relished the simple act of being held by another person, especially by this handsome man whose clasp didn't crush, just held her secure.

"That's good. Now just listen. I can't take away what's been done to you. By the looks of the scars on your back, you've been mistreated."

His low tone soothed the upheaval of her thoughts. In an instant she knew in her heart he wouldn't hurt her. Meanness wasn't part of his spirit. A wave of weariness washed over her and her muscles went lax.

His hand ran the length of her arm in a slow caress. "I don't hurt women. No matter what happens." He fingered her hair, tucking stray tendrils behind her ear. "And I can say that I have never tied one to a bed frame."

Meghan stiffened and twisted to glance over her shoulder. "Sorry."

A chuckle sounded. "Though I might have to reconsider because I can see definite possibilities. Only if both parties are agreeable, that is."

His hold loosened enough that she scooted until she faced him. His leg lowered over hers to keep her still. Nothing in his calm expression made her worry for her safety. "This is your fault, you know."

Bo's eyebrows shot up, and his mouth gaped. "My fault?"

With a tentative move, she lifted her hand to run her fingers along his shadowed jaw. "You showed me kindness."

His eyes widened farther. "And for that I get conked over the head, taken who knows where, and tied up? I don't understand."

Meghan's throat tightened. She ducked her chin, unable to hold his questioning gaze. "Your kindness opened a need deep inside, and I wanted more." A finger lifted her chin until she had to face his dark eyes.

"Tell me what happened. What else did the Indians take?"

Tears welled in her eyes, and this time she let them fall. "My son. The beautiful honey-haired baby that I carried in my body, and then nursed at my breast. For ten months, Little Eagle was my whole life. Everyone loved him. Until the chief's wife got jealous and took him for her own." Her chest felt like it was about to burst, but she wanted Bo to know everything. Swallowing back a sob, she forced out the words. "Then a few months later, my heart was ripped out when he died after falling into the fire during a ceremony." Meghan nestled her cheek against his chest and sobbed out the sorrow that had eaten at her soul for years.

His arm drew her close and rocked her, whispering soothing sounds in her ear.

When she roused, reddish light streamed through the window and the scent of warm male skin tinged with leather filled her nostrils. A rumbling snore sounded close by, and for just a few more seconds, she savored being in Bo's embrace. Then she slipped from under his arm and rolled over the edge to land on her hands and knees. When he didn't move, she found her discarded boots, wrapped her fingers around the knife hilt, and cut the last thong binding him in place.

She would be ever grateful to this man for his part in helping ease her aching heart. With a careful move, she laid the blanket over his exposed legs and walked out the cabin door. The release of her anguish lifted off a weight that she'd barely known had become her life. Everywhere she looked, the colors seemed brighter, the air smelled fresher—and she welcomed the change.

A rustling sounded behind her and with a gasp, she whirled.

Bo stood in the doorway, his hair tousled from sleep and the blanket wrapped around his hips. "My clothes?"

With a smile, she moved to the mesquite bushes where they were drying and gathered them into her arms.

"You washed them? How long was I knocked out?"

"Long enough. Besides I thought I was repaying a service." Heat filled her cheeks, and she held them out.

Instead of taking the clothes, Bo clasped her hand and drew her close. "About that service..."

Her gaze tangled with his, and she saw the heat in his dark eyes that had watched her at the waterfall.

With each statement, he took a backward step, pulling her along. "Yes, I want to touch your breasts. Yes, you are fit. Yes, you are a desirable woman. And hell yes, I want to bed you."

Giving only token resistance, she followed, intrigued by his words.

Bo dumped the clothes on the wooden table, unwrapped the blanket, and stripped off her dress—seemingly all at the same time. He enclosed her in an embrace and lowered his head to capture her mouth in a gentle kiss that explored her lips with soft nibbles.

Meghan stiffened, unused to such soft caresses, and then she relaxed and welcomed the swipe of his probing tongue. Her hand explored his chest and wrapped around his neck.

Then he lifted her, laid her in the middle of the mattress and stood, his gaze taking in her length. A grin spread his lips. "Beautiful."

She looked at him, enjoying the steady rise of his cock. Then looking wasn't enough, and she spread out her arms, beckoning him closer.

Bo covered her body with soft kisses and gentle caresses; he teased her nipples with his swirling tongue, drawing them into the warm cavern of his mouth to suckle her until her back arched off the mattress. His fingers slid along her wet cleft and circled the tight pearl.

Blood pounded through her veins, flowing to all the places on her body where his touch enticed and excited her senses. Never had so many feelings happened inside her before a man entered her body. She pressed her thighs tight and arousal swirled in her pussy. Her hands clamped around Bo's cheeks, and she angled his head from where he kissed her belly. "I want you inside me."

An eyebrow lifted. "Bossy, aren't you?"

His teasing surprised her, and she grinned. In her past experiences, this act had meant only duty. Her fingers ran through his thick hair, urging him closer.

Bo rose over her, his knees spreading her legs, and then his cock pressed against her entrance. With a slow flexing of his hips, he pushed inside until his entire length was sheathed in her tight heat.

A moan slipped from her lips, and Meghan grasped his shoulders. Tingling arousal shot through her pussy. She wrapped her legs around his hips to keep the sensation building. His strength overwhelmed her, and her body slid along the mattress with each powerful stroke.

His mouth covered hers, and his tongue swept inside, inviting her response. With slow strokes, and then with more passion, she tangled her tongue with his until they broke apart breathless.

Gasps filled the air, and they worked in a rhythm that excited and inflamed their senses until fiery ecstasy engulfed her pussy. "Oh, ahhh," she cried out her release, digging her fingernails into his back as her hips still pressed against him.

Then he rolled to his back, his hands clamped on her hips, and pulled her against the length of his cock. His gaze burned with dark desire, and he watched her body move, his features tight with control. A hand stroked her belly and a thumb dipped into the dewy moisture of her release. He brought his hand to his mouth and licked his thumb clean. "Hmm."

Being the object of his attention renewed her arousal. Her heart pumped fast, and she flexed her hips with quick moves. A broad hand cupped her breast, thumbing her nipple and sending zings of pleasure straight to her pussy. When his hands stroked her back, she stiffened and arched away from his touch. No one touched her scars.

"It's okay. I want to touch all of you, Meghan."

His reassuring tone took away her fears. She relinquished herself to the sensations his touch created and her orgasm hit, stealing her breath.

Bo rose, placed her feet flat on the mattress, and embraced her back, grunting as he powered in his last thrusts and let out a resounding groan of satisfaction.

Meghan dropped her forehead to his shoulder and reveled in the glow of their lovemaking. He eased them down to the mattress and covered them with the blanket.

Hours later, the flap of a bird's wings woke Meghan. The scent of coffee filled the air, and she opened to eyes to see Bo outlined by the breaking dawn. "Heading out?"

"Work to be done."

She struggled to sit up. "Here, let me cut off that thong."

"Don't. I'm keeping it."

"Why?"

"To remind me who binds my heart."

BACKSTAGE PASS

Cynthia D'Alba

I glanced around my assigned hotel suite with a mixture of awe and gratitude. While I might have given myself the birthday trip to Las Vegas to see Cody Jarrod—my absolute favorite country singer—in concert, my bank account couldn't have begun to pay for these accommodations.

The plush one-bedroom corner suite with floor-to-ceiling windows, offering a 180-degree panoramic view of the Las Vegas strip with all its gaudy loveliness, was a birthday present from my best friend, Leslie. Fifteen hundred square feet. Deep-pile beige carpet. Enormous living room with overstuffed sofas and chairs. Dining table for six. Master bedroom with a raised platform, king-sized bed and thousand-thread-count sheets. Marble master bathroom with a two-person whirlpool and a glass-enclosed shower. It boggled my mind to imagine all the wicked things I could do in this suite if only I had someone to do them with...and maybe I would.

My friends worried about my solo travel to Vegas. I'd tried to convince everyone that I was fine alone. However, I had to admit I'd gone through a sex dry spell. It wasn't entirely my fault. Real men couldn't hold a candle to my fantasy man, Cody Jarrod.

I made my way back to the bar in the living room where Krug champagne chilled on the bar's marble top, icy drops of sweat running down the neck. I turned the bottle a couple of times while I studied the nibbles hotel catering had supplied—fresh strawberries, whipped cream, grapes, small sandwiches and a cake. Being a foodie, I was in heaven, but my friends had promised me there would be more to the evening than food and liquor.

Leslie had planned something special to make this a birthday to remember. I worried a little about her gift. One of her fantasies was sex with a professional male escort. A man who knew his way around the female body. I'd told her she'd watched Richard Gere in *American Gigolo* too many times. She'd laughed and told me to answer the door and enjoy the evening.

I twisted out the cork on the Krug champagne and filled a crystal flute. My hand shook a little as I lifted the glass to my lips.

While she'd never confirmed my guess, I knew Leslie well enough to suspect she was indeed sending a male escort to my room for the night. While I was nervous about the idea, my dry spell had gone on long enough. I was getting a man who knew his way around a woman's body. Could there be a better present...or better friend?

I moved to the windows, taking my champagne with me, and watched the flashing neon lights of the strip. From this height, they all looked like gems winking under the fluorescent lights of a jewelry store.

A doorbell rang, and I startled. Sudden awareness of what I was doing dampened my thong with arousal juices. Could I have sex with a stranger, no matter how professional he was?

The breath caught in my lungs at my first glance into the hall.

Dressed in worn jeans that cupped his groin like a lover's hand, a yoked snap shirt, and holding a cowboy hat in one hand stood the man my friend had hired for the evening. The lips surrounding my pussy swelled in response.

His brown hair fell in silky strands of waves and curls along his neck and behind his ears. One lock hung casually over his brow, and I clenched my fingers to keep from pushing it back.

My friend had found Cody Jarrod's doppelganger as my evening fuck. My fantasy combined with hers. *Thank you, Leslie.*

Piercing green eyes glanced at me, the only difference between this guy and the real Cody Jarrod. I'd read his eyes were hazel, but the rest of him was dead-on perfect. The man looked down at the piece of paper in his hand.

"Are you Faith Myers?" His deep voice was thick with a Southern accent, not exactly a match to Cody Jarrod's voice but close enough for me. His chiseled cheeks brandished a five o'clock shadow, a style the country singer was known for. The thought of the gentle scratch of that beard against my inner thighs sent a shiver running down my spine.

My gaze slid from that delicious curl over his brow down to broad shoulders and a firm chest covered by a shirt that seemed to beg to be unsnapped. Yeah, I could do that. I let my eyes roam down to a set of dusty, worn cowboy boots. I smiled. This guy had gone all out to fulfill my fantasy.

"Faith Myers?"

"Oh, yes. Sorry. Come on in. Call me Faith, please."

The Cody clone folded up the piece of paper he'd been reading and shoved it into the front pocket of his jeans. I stuck my hand in his waistband and pulled him through the door.

"I—"

I placed my fingers over his lips. "I know who you are. " My insides hummed with anticipation. Dampness seeped between my thighs. Now that I'd seen my birthday present, my fingers itched to unwrap it.

He grinned, which didn't exactly match the smile I'd seen Cody use onstage, but again, close enough to shoot my libido through the ceiling. "Great. Then you know why I'm here."

"I do, and I'll admit I was a little hesitant about the whole idea but..." I shrugged. "Once I got used to the idea, I've been looking forward to meeting you all day."

His mouth quirked at the corner. "Well, I'm always happy to meet a fan. I believe I'm supposed to tell you happy birthday and give you a birthday kiss."

I almost laughed. Oh yeah, I'd take that kiss. It just wouldn't be on my face. "Would you like a glass of champagne, Cody?" I almost choked on the name. For a minute, I wondered what his real name was. Of course, it didn't matter.

"Been a long time since I've had champagne. Most of the time it's beer or whiskey," he said, keeping up the cowboy country singer persona. I appreciated his efforts.

"So, how do we go about this?" I asked, handing him a flute of Krug.

"This?" He took the glass, a ripple of confusion rolling across his face.

"Just stand there a second," I said. "I want to get a good look before you get naked."

He choked on the champagne he'd just sipped. "Naked?"

I walked around him, taking a couple of extra seconds to admire his ass in those tight jeans.

"Well, it *is* my birthday, so I think I should get to see you naked," I said as I completed my visual tour of my present.

"Don't you? Or am I moving too fast? I've never been with a male, er, professional escort before." I gulped down my champagne. "I mean, you look like Cody Jarrod...a lot. You don't have his voice or speech pattern down pat, but I'll give your agency credit. They did an awesome job finding you for me."

"Finding me?" His brow furled. "Professional what?"

"I'm sorry. I know you're the professional escort, but I'd rather be upfront." I drank my champagne for courage. "I've had a little, um, dry spell, sexually. My friends hired you, hoping you can put an end to that."

Cody's Adam's apple moved up and down as he drained his champagne flute. "Well, this isn't what I expected," he murmured.

I smiled. "Like I said, I'm not really sure how to proceed. Is this right?" I jerked his shirttail from his jeans and pulled the ends apart until the snaps began to pop open.

Cody's eyes widened.

I loved that he was playing along with my little game. As I reached for the hat he still held, it dawned on me what was going on, why he was letting me make the advances. Obviously, he'd been warned I might be a little shy and uncomfortable at first, seeing as this was my first time with a paid escort. He was letting me set the pace.

I pulled the Stetson from his hand and leaned over the sofa to set it crown-side down. Looking over my shoulder, I bit my lip as I noticed his gaze taking in my ass.

His nostrils flared as he drew in a breath. "Look, Faith, I..."

I stood and turned. Dipping my head, I ran my tongue from his jean's waistband, stopping to circle his navel. When my tongue's tip filled that cavity, his stomach sucked in with a gasp. His fingers threaded through my hair. My breasts pressed into his groin. His zipper bulged with his hard cock.

I congratulated myself. I must have done something right if I was able to get a professional aroused so quickly.

Continuing the slide of my tongue, I circled his nipples, now matching his dick in rigidity. I licked the hollow at the base of his throat before starting my trip back down. When I reached the waistband of his jeans, I pressed my nose against his flesh and let his spicy scent fill my senses. Moving my mouth down, I caught his jeans-covered cock between my teeth. The fingers in my hair tightened, pulling me closer.

I stood and pushed the white fabric shirt off his shoulders. His skin was tanned and smooth, and his muscles firm and hard. They tensed and jumped under my hands as I stroked. The nerve endings in my fingers tingled.

I craved the taste of him again. I drew his nipple into my mouth, caressed the small rigid nub between my teeth with a light bite, then ran my tongue around his flat, brown disk.

"Wait, Faith. I'm not who you think I am."

I looked into his eyes. The beautiful emerald-green irises were now dark and glowing with desire. "Oh, hell yeah. I know who and what you are," I said with a grin. "A lady should always get what she wants for her birthday. And I want to fuck Cody Jarrod for my birthday. You wouldn't deny me my gift, would you?"

God, this game was fun. I loved how he played his role to perfection.

He shrugged and yanked my blouse over my head before tossing it across the room to a chair. "I can certainly see your point."

His large hands seized my breasts, the heat from his palms radiating through my pink lace bra as he fondled, pulling and rolling my nipples between his fingers. I dropped my head back and groaned.

My nipples hardened, aching with need. He continued to torture me by rubbing his palms back and forth across the lace, drawing my nipples painfully erect with desire, my breasts hungry for his mouth.

Wrapping an arm around my waist, he leaned me backward, arching my back and thrusting my breasts up. I sizzled as his scorching mouth suckled me through the lace while pinching the other nipple between firm fingers.

"Touch me," I demanded. "Suck me. I have to feel your mouth on my flesh."

The front clasp on my bra snapped open. My overheated flesh met the cool room air for only a second before he ran his tongue around the nipple.

"Magnificent," he said on a sigh and sucked my breast deep into his sultry mouth.

My pussy twitched and throbbed, demanding its share of attention.

I cupped his erection through the crotch of his jeans. His rigid length filled my hand. I wanted to touch him, feel that cock in my mouth.

I unfastened his belt, pulling the leather slowly through the denim loops. When I reached the end, I coiled the strip of leather on the floor by his feet.

"Since today is your day, why don't I give you that birthday kiss I promised?" He grabbed my hand and pulled me over to the dining table. He unhooked my skirt, letting it slide to the floor, exposing my black thong.

He groaned and covered my ass with rough hands and squeezed. "Oh, baby. Nice."

He hoisted me onto the table. The slick mahogany chilled my bottom, but did nothing to control the furnace raging inside me. Cody dropped to his knees, wedged his shoulders between my thighs, and drew in a deep breath. A warm gust heated the crotch of my panties, already soaked with my juices. I leaned back on my elbows, thrilling in the sight of chestnut curls between my pale thighs.

His nose pressed against my crotch, pressing the soaked silk into my slit. Cool air filtered between my folds as he sniffed. "You smell wonderful. I bet you taste even better. Lift your hips," he growled, just before jerking my thong over them and down my legs.

I knew he had to see the secretions dripping from my cunt toward my ass, secretions that begged to be tasted. He stood, pushed my legs farther apart, fully exposing my lips and pussy for his perusal. My toes curled as I pressed my ass firmly against the table to restrain myself from pushing into his face and demanding he drink.

"Damn you're wet," he said with a self-satisfied smile. "I know what would go perfect with all your cream. More cream." He reached for the bowl of whipped cream, dipped his fingers and smeared the cold, smooth substance over my pussy.

A shiver ran up my spine and then down to the soles of my feet. My cunt gushed in response. He dropped the bowl and grabbed my birthday cake. Pulling off a piece, he spread white cake over the whipped cream covering my sex.

"I'm sure you'll be the best birthday cake I've ever eaten. Now, don't move while I give you that kiss I promised."

He pushed me flat on the table, and for the first time I noticed the mirrored ring surrounding the chandelier. I watched as he started at my breasts, licking, sucking and nibbling. Each rasp of tongue on my flesh sent electrical shock waves through my veins. Each nibble was met with an arching of my back. He was torturing me with his mouth. He knew it and I knew it, but my lord, what sweet torture it was.

He reached my navel and his tongue delved in, swirling around and around until I cried out. "I can't stand any more. I need you to eat me. Now."

He tsked with a grin. "I think I saw you move. Naughty girl. I'll have to fix that."

He walked away, leaving my legs spread wide open, whipped cream and cake coating my pussy. I started to sit up, but I didn't. This man was a pro, not a date. This was his job. He knew what he was doing. He knew what I needed even if I didn't.

A minute later, he was back. He pulled my left ankle to the side. Cool silk stroked my ankle as he tied my robe tie snuggly. My left thigh muscle stretched as he secured the tie to a table leg. Then cool leather wrapped around my right ankle seconds before as he secured it to another table leg. He stood back and inspected his work. I was pulled tight, spread as far as my legs could go. Next, he tied my hands together with my thong and secured my arms to the chair at my head with my bra. I tugged at my restraints but nothing moved.

My pussy throbbed with excitement. Creamy fluid flooded from me as I realized the situation. I was naked, tied to a table, covered in cake and cream, and my cowboy fantasy was standing there taking it all in. I pulled against the ties, rubbing my ass against the slick wood.

He dropped to his knees again. His shoulders jammed between my thighs. He pressed his mouth over my slit and sucked my sex into his mouth.

"Oh, shit," I moaned, trying to shove more of me into his mouth. "More. More."

His tongue darted out, licking the cake and cream from my slit. My hips wiggled. My bones liquefied as his tongue flicked and licked, cleaning every crevice.

I rolled my head on the table, overcome with the flood of feelings surging through my system. Pressure was building inside, my orgasm coming on like a freight train. "Cody. Stop. I can't take any more."

He ignored me, thrusting his tongue inside my pussy and sucking my lips into his mouth. His fingers traced around my sensitive nub, not touching it, just hinting what it might feel like if he did.

"Suck my clit. Damn it. Suck my clit," I gasped. "I need to come."

"Not yet. Hold it," he growled and circled my clit with his mouth. He bit down, and I cried out. He soothed the biting pain with his tongue, lapping around and over my nub.

My hips arched off the table and my restraints pulled tight, holding me spread wide for him. He pushed a finger inside me, then added a second, thrusting them in and out in time with the thrusts of his tongue.

Then a finger found my anus, a totally virgin area. He pressed a thick finger against that hole.

I froze, not sure what to do. Slowly he pushed his finger in. My ass burned from the intrusion. He bit my clit again. When I arched in response, he pushed his finger up to the knuckle.

"Damn. Damn," I chanted.

The finger in my ass began to rotate, stretching tissue that'd never felt such a touch.

"Damn. Fuck me," I demanded.

He gave a low, throaty laugh. "I'm not ready to fuck you, but I'll give you something to cool you off."

Something icy cold touched my abdomen for a second before cold champagne trickled over my pelvis and down between my folds. Cody's mouth was positioned to catch the champagne, now infused with my creamy fluid.

"That help?" he asked with a smirk.

Help? Hell, it raised my temperature and shot volts of adrenaline racing through my bloodstream.

"We're almost out of champagne. I wonder what the bellhop would say if he delivered more and found you stretched out like this? Would you like that? Would you like for other men to see you like this? They can, you know." He nodded toward the floor-to-ceiling windows.

I'd forgotten about those.

"Anyone can see in here. See you spread and pulled tight. Is that what you want?"

I shivered from excitement and arousal. I licked my lips and croaked out, "Cody."

"You'd like that, wouldn't you? Of course, since I'm so famous, I've made sure to keep my face turned away from any prying eyes." He chuckled as he picked up the telephone on the bar and punched some buttons. "Yes, we need another bottle of Krug. No, make that two more bottles. Yes, I need them delivered immediately," he said, staring me in the eyes, daring me to object. "Thank you." He hung up. "Room service is on the way."

He drank the last of the Krug and twirled the neck of the bottle in the ice water. "But I think we can still have some fun with this empty." He traced my slit with the icy neck of the bottle a couple of times.

I hissed and moaned. "Fuck."

He twirled the bottle in the ice water again. I expected him to rub me again, but instead, he slid the frigid glass dildo inside me. My pussy throbbed against the intrusion. The bottle was so cold, and I was so hot. My cream coated the makeshift dildo as Cody fucked me. I rocked my hips in time to the rhythm he set, letting my climax come closer. As I neared the peak, the doorbell rang.

Cody pulled the bottle from me and grinned. "More champagne for the birthday girl. Do you want me to let the server through the door? He could lick you, too. We both could take you at once. Would you like that? One in your cunt and one up your ass? Or I could watch as he fucked you raw." .

I shook my head. "No. Just you. Just you, anywhere you want."

He gave me that satisfied smirk again, letting me know he was enjoying my torment, and went to the door. He didn't let the server in. I don't know if the guy could see into the room or if my pussy reflected off the windows, but just the thought sent a torrent of liquid from me.

Cody came back and shoved both bottles into the ice. "I decided not to share. But I think you've waited long enough, birthday girl." He stood between my legs and pushed three fingers into my cunt. He pumped them at a rapid pace while squeezing and rolling my clit between the thumb and forefinger of his other hand. Each pinch of my nub, each plunge of his fingers inside me sent rivulets of electricity, pushing me higher and higher. I came in a burst of dizzying tension, jerking against my restraints, letting the ripples of pleasure race up and down my spine.

When the final wave of pleasure passed, I shuddered in completion and lay there enjoying the aftershocks and tingles.

Cody untied me, wrapped my legs around his waist and pulled me to a sitting position.

"That was nice," I purred.

"Nice? Hell, we're just getting started."

I quivered in anticipation. "Then I think you need to get dressed for our party," I said, shoving my hand between our bodies, stroking his hard dick through his jeans.

He lowered my legs, took one step back and unzipped his pants. My breathing grew more rapid as I waited. My mouth salivated. I know some women give blow jobs because the guy likes it. I give blow jobs because *I* love it—the intoxicating aroma of male musk, the salty taste of flesh, the tang of his precome, the rasp of coarse pubic hair on my tongue. I quivered just thinking about it and more liquid cream trickled onto the table.

He pushed the denim and his briefs to the floor in one motion. My gaze took in his long, hard dick rising from the thatch of curly brown hair, and I swallowed. His cock was huge and meaty, and I couldn't wait to get my lips around it. I wiggled off the table and stood.

"Wait a minute," he said, toeing off his boots. He tossed his clothes into a chair.

I grabbed his wrist and pulled him over to the sofa. I shoved him down and dropped to my knees between his legs. His thick shaft bobbed toward my mouth as though taunting me, exciting me to the point of starvation. I do love a playful dick.

"Since you're so famous and all," I said before I ran my tongue around the head, dipping into the slit, sucking his precome onto my lips. "Your back is to the window. Your identity is secure." I licked along the thick penile vein until I reached the spongy head again. The milky fluid was exquisite, bursting with that pungent, salty zest I craved. I heard Cody moan, but I didn't take the time to look up. Instead, my lips circled the head of his penis, and I sucked, pulling just the smooth silky head into my mouth. I love that little ridge just below the head before I get to the shaft, but doesn't everybody? I nibbled around the rim, savoring the feel of his taut skin between my teeth and the gasps I heard.

His fingers made tracks through my hair; they tightened, pulling my hair to keep my face close to his groin. The pain in my scalp only served to heighten my excitement.

Opening wider, I slid him into my mouth, my jaws stretching to accommodate his massive girth. When he hit the back of my throat, I pulled my head back, applying forceful suction and dragging my teeth along the shaft.

"Damn," he said, hissing breath between his clenched teeth and spreading his knees farther apart. "Deeper," he ordered. "Pretend I'm that famous singer you keep talking about. How would you do him?"

"Scoot down," I said.

And he did, giving me better access to his balls. Now, as much as I love a thick, meaty cock in my mouth, the sensation of rolling a man's balls between my lips makes me wet.

I slid my finger in my mouth and then under his sac, watching his balls move to separate sides. I leaned over and traced the same path with my tongue. The skin there was soft and slippery. The sparse, coarse hair tickled my face. Sucking one ball between my lips, I rolled the other around and around in my hand, delighting in his weight and texture. My tongue lapped at the ball in my mouth.

Moisture dripped down my leg. My pussy demanded attention, but my mouth wasn't ready to give up its prize.

I swirled my tongue around the base of his cock, then up his shaft until I reached the velvety head. I sucked off more precome, and then slid him into my mouth. This time, I didn't stop at the back of my throat. I swallowed, took him deep, deep enough that my teeth circled the base of his penis. Coarse pubic hair scraped my lips.

He held my head firmly, not allowing me to move. His hips came alive, thrusting up and deeper into my throat.

"You realize," he said with a powerful thrust into my mouth, "that we're in front of windows in all directions. Anyone could see you like this, naked, at my feet, doing what I tell you to do. In fact, there are probably ten guys watching right now as I fuck your mouth. Ten guys with their dicks in their hands imagining your mouth on them…" He pulled back and thrust again. "Dying to fuck your mouth like I am, wanting to fuck your cunt like I will."

My pussy contracted, spilling thick juice down my legs. I reached between my legs, fingering myself to his words, pressing against my clit.

He jerked his dick from my mouth. "That's enough," he said, his voice rough and gravelly. He stood, and for a minute, I panicked. I thought he was leaving.

"Where are you going?"

Retrieving his pants from the chair, he removed a packet. Quickly rolling on a condom, he crooked his finger. "Come here. I want to show all those guys watching just what they're missing."

I went to him. He wrapped a large hand around the back of my neck and bent me over the sofa. Thick, heavy baroque material abraded my rigid nipples as I rubbed against it, not caring who saw.

"Spread your legs," he said.

I did.

"Wider," he whispered in my ear. "How do you expect all those other guys to see your pretty pink pussy with your legs so close together?"

I obeyed, then looked over my shoulder, awaiting his approval.

He traced a finger along my slit, coating it with my juices, then sucked his finger into his mouth. "You taste like honey," he said. He did it again, licking my juices from his hand. "All those other men watching. They can only guess what you taste like. I know."

My breaths came in ragged gasps. I'd never been more wet and ready to be fucked in my life. "Fuck me, dammit."

Cody turned his back to the window, grabbed my hips and drove deep inside in one push.

I gasped as my walls stretched to accommodate his size. He withdrew and stabbed me again. It felt as though his cock touched the back of my throat. Everything inside me moved with each thrust. My heart pounded and raced.

"Turn your head to the right," he said as he withdrew.

I did. The room's mirrored wall shot our reflections back to us. He plunged into me, and I watched his massive cock spread my lips and disappear inside me. Oh god. I'd never watched myself being fucked before. My legs quivered. When he pulled back, my cream covered him. I moaned, arching my back and shoving my ass into his groin.

"Harder. Faster," I said. The pressure inside was building and I was close to coming. "Faster, harder."

He pumped into me, slamming me against the back of the sofa.

"Don't stop," I gasped out. "I'm—" My orgasm hit me like a tsunami. Multicolored flashes lit up my sight as ripple after ripple of pleasure raced through my body.

While I was trying to regain my senses, Cody slammed into me a couple more times before he ground his pelvis into my ass. His cock jerked inside as he came.

We both stayed in that position, trying to catch our breaths. In a minute, he withdrew, taking all his warmth with him.

"Excuse me," he said and went to the half bath off the entry hall. I remained draped over the chair for a moment, concerned my legs would falter if I tried to walk. But I didn't want him to come back and find me like that. I went to the master bedroom and tossed on the silk robe missing a tie. When I came back out, Cody was snapping his shirt, finishing dressing.

I leaned against the door jam. "Happy birthday to me," I said. I'm sure I wore a wide smile.

He came over and kissed me. "Happy birthday."

I realized this was the first time we'd kissed. He had a nice kiss. His soft, full lips cushioned the kiss, making it gentle and sweet.

"I have to go," he said.

I nodded. He probably had another client tonight. I wasn't jealous, per se, but I hoped he was too tired to do her and had to cancel. I know. Bad of me.

I walked him to the door, and he kissed me again. "That was a hell of a lot of fun. You are incredible," he said. "I hope this will be a birthday you'll remember."

"Without a doubt," I said, and smiled. "Thank you."

He took my hand and kissed it. "Thank *you*."

He left, and I leaned against the door. Damn. How in the hell would I top this for Leslie's birthday next month? I stuck my hand in my robe pocket and felt cardboard. Pulling it out, I was shocked to find a front-row ticket for that night's Cody Jarrod concert and a backstage pass.

Cody Jarrod whistled as he headed back to his room. Damn, that had been fun. Nobody would ever believe he'd been mistaken for a professional gigolo playing Cody Jarrod. He wondered what new role he could play tonight when he knocked on Faith Meyers's door.

UNFINISHED BUSINESS

Cat Johnson

I can't believe you talked me into going to this thing." Skye Morrison stared at the building glowing like Mecca across the parking lot.

"Oh, hush up. It's going to be fun." Libby locked the car door and turned toward the bar.

"But the Spittoon? Seriously, the committee couldn't have booked the golf club? Or at least rented the legion hall?" Who held a reunion at a honky-tonk? Apparently, the Norman High School graduating class of 2003 did. Only in Oklahoma...

"God, remember that night we got our fake IDs and came here?" Libby sighed. "It feels so long ago."

Skye followed her friend as they picked their way across the poorly lit, gravel lot. "Of course, I remember. And it *was* long ago."

But not so long ago that Skye had forgotten that night or *him*. She and Libby had driven all the way out here so they wouldn't run into anyone who'd know they were three years too young to be drinking. The thrill of sneaking around and playing at being older had infected Skye, made her reckless. She'd ended the night pressed between the bed of a pickup and the hard body of the local cowboy who owned the truck, while Libby was inside with his best friend.

Rowdy Reynolds. All these years later, Skye not only remembered her cowboy's name; thinking it still made her tingle. He was her first real, grown-up kiss. Her first orgasm too. No, they hadn't gone all the way, but damn, that man knew how to touch a woman. He'd shown her exactly what he could do with only half an hour and his hand. The pleasure had nearly taken Skye off her feet, and had ruined her for all men since. It seemed she'd yet to find that kind of desperate passion she'd felt with Rowdy all those years ago.

And now here she was, ten years older, hopefully a whole lot wiser, but back at the Spittoon where she'd have to smile at a bunch of people she hadn't seen or thought about in years. She was tempted to turn tail and run. "I'm so not in the mood for this."

Libby reached for the door handle "You've been working in the city too long. It's made you antisocial. Relax. You're not going to be trapped with anyone you don't like. We've got the private back room where they're setting up the food and cake, but we can still go up front to dance and enjoy the band with the regular crowd."

That was something, anyway. Skye let out a huff of breath. "All right."

Libby rolled her eyes and then opened the door. As the combined din of the music and the many patrons hit Skye, her first thought was that the bar was loud enough that she'd have a good excuse to not talk at all if she didn't want to.

Maybe Libby was right and she was getting antisocial, but as a guy carrying a pitcher splashed beer all over her, Skye figured she had a right to be.

Crap. Hell of start to the night.

"I've got beer all over me." She had to yell to Libby to be heard. "I'm going to the bar to get napkins."

"Okay. I'm going to see who's here." Libby hooked a thumb toward the back as she shouted.

Skye nodded and wedged her way between the people. It wasn't easy, and by the time she got to the bar, she'd already had enough of this place—but then she saw him, silhouetted by neon.

She stopped, her hand poised in midair as she reached for the stack of white napkins. It couldn't be. Could it?

He turned, took one look at her face and his baby blues crinkled with his smile. "It's you."

Skye let out a breathless laugh as the tenor of Rowdy's voice vibrated through her. "And it's you too."

"Good to see you again, darlin'." He knocked back the hat hiding his dark hair and leaned in, laying his hand on her arm as he brushed a kiss against her cheek. Pulling back, he grinned and reached for a handful of napkins. "You've already been christened, I see."

He daubed at her wet skin, wiping the beer away. A drop had landed on her chest. He brushed that away too as Skye realized that just a moment with this man had her getting wet elsewhere. She wouldn't have been surprised if he felt the thundering of her heart through that napkin.

What the hell was it about this guy? She wasn't an eighteen-year-old virgin pretending to be twenty-one anymore. She'd knocked off the dust of her small town and moved on to bigger and better things. Skye had a great job and her own apartment. She'd had boyfriends. She'd had sex.

Of course, not sex like it would be with him. Skye felt the truth of that to her core. Whether it was pheromones or memories of that brief moment they'd shared ten years ago, she didn't know. All she could be sure of was that she had a visceral reaction to this man now.

Meanwhile, he probably didn't even remember her name. His *darlin'* was charming, but it could also hide the fact he didn't know what else to call her. But when he deposited the used napkins on the bar and turned the full attention of his charm back to her, Skye realized she didn't give a damn if he knew her name or not. He'd recognized her, and he remembered all they'd done—the look in his eyes told her that much. And that was enough for her.

From beneath her lashes, she gazed up at this man who towered over her, making her feel small, but in a good way. "Hey, you wanna get out of here?"

His brows rose at her suggestion, disappearing beneath the brim of his hat briefly before he dipped his head in a nod. "Sure. Where you wanna go?"

"You still got that truck of yours?"

The dimple in his chin caught her eye as he smiled. "Not the same one, but I do have a truck parked out back. This one's got a king cab. Lots of room."

The tip of his tongue shot out and swiped across his lips, causing Skye to focus on his mouth and thoughts of what it could do to her. "Sounds good. Let's go."

His eyes widened before he nodded. "All right."

Rowdy pushed his beer bottle toward the bartender, then turned and took Skye's hand in his. She'd forgotten he was a hand holder. He'd led her outside in exactly this manner those many years ago, but this time she wasn't going to leave with unfinished business.

The feel of his thick, rough fingers wrapped around hers was only a preview of things to come. She anticipated what his hands would feel like running over her bare skin. The thought started a flutter low in her belly. What she wouldn't give for a nice big bed right now. For the first time ever, Skye wished she still lived in her hometown, instead of outside of Oklahoma City where she worked.

Out in the cool night air, Skye ran a hand along the sleek sides of the vehicle. The truck matched the man—big, strong, nice to look at and they both could take a girl places.

He paused next to the passenger side door and gazed down. Raising one hand, he cupped her cheek and leaned low. He stopped just shy of her mouth. "It's been a long time."

Her gaze met his. "Then we best not waste any more of it."

A crooked smile bowed his lips right before he closed the distance and pressed them against hers. He might play it slow and cool, but his actions told a different story. Rowdy's tongue slid between her lips to tangle with hers a moment after they made contact. He was as eager as she to get back to what they'd started all those years ago.

Still kissing her, Rowdy fumbled inside the front pocket of his jeans. The locks of the truck doors clicked. Blindly, he reached for the handle and opened the door. With his hands wrapped around Skye's waist, he broke the kiss only long enough to sit her sideways, facing him in the seat.

He stepped closer to stand between her legs. His hands came to rest on each of her thighs as he leaned in again for one more kiss. Skye realized how fortuitous it was she'd chosen to wear a dress when his hands slid higher beneath the hem.

Maybe her mind had exaggerated the memory of how good his touch had felt that first and only time. She could only hope, even though she feared Rowdy would be even harder to walk away from at the end of the night now than he had been back then.

Deft in his movements, he slipped one digit beneath the edge of her panties and zeroed in on her clit.

Skye drew in a sharp breath.

Rowdy smiled. "Still sensitive, I see."

Her only answer was the tilt of her hips that pressed her more firmly against his finger. He chuckled at the move and increased both the speed and the pressure of his touch. Skye's nails scraped against the seat and the dashboard, seeking something to grab on to as her body coiled for release.

Thank goodness he'd parked in the deserted back corner of the lot where it bordered the woods. She was so close to something she knew would be amazing, she'd die if he had to stop because someone walked over.

He worked her hard and fast until the first wave of pleasure crashed over her. Skye's hips bucked against his hand as the orgasm began. He didn't stop, but rode it out until the end. Even once the spasms ended, he didn't. Rowdy slid one finger inside her and stroked this thumb over nerves so sensitive she jumped as if electric current flowed between them.

Smiling, he withdrew his touch.

She missed it, immediately. Skye gasped for breath but still wanted more. "Don't stop now."

"Darlin', sex with you deserves a bed." Rowdy glanced at the open back of the pickup. "And I don't mean the bed of my truck."

"I don't know about that. There's something to be said for being out here. Alone together, so close to all those people." She ran a fingertip down his shirt, not stopping until she hit his belt buckle.

Rowdy's gaze followed her path before he dragged his focus

up to her face. "You like playing at being bad, don't you? Just like that night you were here pretending you were old enough to drink."

Skye frowned. "You knew? And you weren't that much older than us."

"I was at least legal. Your friend told my friend, but even if she hadn't I knew from one look that you were a good girl out for a wild night." He yanked her hips to the very edge of the seat so her legs straddled his. "I didn't give it to you then. You sure you can handle it now?"

They were so close that, positioned as they were, if they'd been naked he'd be inside her. The thought had her heart pounding harder, as did the sight of his hands resting on his belt buckle, paused, waiting for her answer.

"Yes. I can handle it."

That, apparently, was all he needed to hear.

"Lie back." He gave the order and had the buckle open and the two sides of his jeans hanging open by the time her head hit the bench seat. Skye watched as he freed his erection from his cotton briefs. Big and thick, just like she'd envisioned so many times.

While looking down, he pushed inside her, slow but firm. He hissed in a breath as he inched deeper. "So damn tight."

He was big, and she certainly wasn't used to that from the last guy she'd been serious enough about to sleep with, but she was wetter than ever. Rowdy worked his way in until his cock was fully seated. He set a steady rhythm that began slow, but soon sped up. Every stroke made her feel completely taken. Filled. Possessed.

The sight of the cowboy thrusting into her, the pure bliss on his face nearly hidden by the shadow of his hat and the night around them, had Skye's body clenching.

Reaching out, he pulled her toward him. He tangled one hand in her hair and buried his face near her ear, and she felt his labored breathing. He was close. So was she. The tingling began and increased until she was panting as much as he was.

She clamped her arms and legs around him and held tight as the second orgasm of the night hit, even more amazing than the first because he was inside her for it. He stiffened against her, thrust deep and held. Her muscles gripped his cock, clenching around him, milking his release from him.

They stayed wrapped around each other, him still inside her, for too long considering where they were. He moved first, pulling out, and glanced down between them. He grabbed napkins from the dashboard, and for the second time that night, wiped her clean. This man she barely knew, yet knew intimately.

"Little late to ask, I know, but is it okay that I came inside you?"

"Yes, it is a little late." Skye cocked one brow. "But yes, it's okay."

"Good." He nodded. He watched her straighten her underwear and skirt as he fastened his pants and belt.

"I guess I should get inside. My friend's waiting." She moved to climb down from the high seat.

He stepped closer to block her way. "I want to see you again."

"That's very nice of you to say, but we both know what this was." Skye laughed. "You probably don't even know my name."

He leaned close and whispered, "Skye. How could I forget? You're as beautiful as the night sky over Oklahoma."

She drew in a breath. "You remembered."

"I haven't forgotten a thing about you." He pressed a kiss to her neck. "You're likely the reason why no woman I've dated over the past decade has held my interest. At least not for the long haul. Why do you think I still come here every Saturday night even though I moved to the next county years ago?"

"In case I came back?" she asked, hope making her breathless.

"Yes and you sure took your time doing it." He trailed kisses down her throat. "So I guess the question is, after all these years, do you remember my name?"

"I haven't forgotten a thing about you either, Rowdy Reynolds, blacksmith apprentice who wanted to own his own ranch one day." She pressed her lips against the stubble at the corner of his mouth.

His eyes narrowed. "Hearing you say that makes me want you all over again. One time with you isn't enough."

He wasn't kidding. He was hard again. She felt it through the stiff denim of his jeans.

"How about the whole night?" she asked.

"It's a start." His voice came out low and full of promise.

"Then we'll start with tonight and see where we go from there." Skye had a feeling they'd go directly to his bed, but that wasn't such a bad place to begin.

AT THE
MERCY OF THE
COWBOY

Amber Lin

O nly when the squinty-eyed, scruff-jawed cowboy scowls do I feel guilty for my deception. I had signed my email *Alex*, which isn't strictly a lie since that's my name. But of course he assumed it was a man applying for his live-in farmhand job, which is why he sent back a terse email with his address and the line: *Come ready to work.*

"You can't have the job." There's no softness at all in his gruff voice, in the sloping lines of his body. His silhouette slices through the swath of sunset backdrop. An orange glow spills around his edges, leaving his face in shadows. Even dark and half-hidden, the answer is written plainly: *No.*

"Why not?" I challenge. "I can work hard. You'll see."

"I won't, because you're not staying. It's physical labor. Back-breaking labor for a man in his prime, and you look like a stiff wind would knock you over." As if to prove his point, his perfunctory glance slides over my threadbare clothes and now-thin body. Just as easily, he looks away in dismissal, painting his side profile with light, a straight nose and stubble-roughened jaw.

"Let me try. What can it hurt? If I can't cut it, I'll leave all on my own."

"The room's right next to mine. It's more of a closet, really. Not fit for a..."

"I'm not picky."

"No."

I would have just left then. Under ordinary circumstances, I wouldn't even be anywhere near a ranch in the little town of Paloma, Kansas. But there are no jobs in Topeka. I've looked and looked, and now I'm desperate.

"Please," I say.

As if just noticing it, he glances over to my twelve-year-old, forest-green station wagon. I flush hotly, but he doesn't see, because he's looking instead at the boxes in the backseat, piled high with clothes and old family photo albums I couldn't bear to throw away.

I'm a grown woman, but I had never realized how close I was to homelessness. Just a layoff, a fruitless job search and an eviction notice away from ruin. My parents had long since passed away, and I had no friends close enough to put me up indefinitely. In truth, I'd been too ashamed to ask. I want to work. I *need* this job.

And now he knows it.

Thick eyebrows lower beneath the brim of his mottled-beige cowboy hat. His eyes are nothing more than slits in the simmering sun. Beneath thick work jeans and a plaid button-down, he seems tense. Or maybe that's just me. I brace myself for the feel of his cowboy boot as he kicks my ass out.

"You can stay," he says. "Start with shoveling out the stalls."

He expects me to balk, I can tell. He doesn't elaborate on the task or show me where to get started. Just stands there, waiting for me to tell him that shit-shoveling is beneath me. But what's really beneath me is charity. If this is what I've come to, then at least my meals will be honestly earned.

I summon a smile. "Great."

With a snort, he strides to the stable, a large building set twenty feet from the house. After a few minutes of rustling and the click of a latch, he emerges leading a tall brown horse with white on its snout. Very tall. It matches the man, and they both tower above me as they pass—intimidating. Just another way to make a point against me, to show I don't belong, another way to say *no*. But I won't be discouraged. Desperation imbues me with strength, and I channel all my frustration and hope into the physical, backbreaking work.

Colt—that's the cowboy's name—likes to think of himself as a hard-ass. And he is, but I figure out almost immediately that he has a soft spot for starving, out-of-work administrative assistants named Alexis Walker.

On the very first night, he informs me in his take-no-prisoners tone that food is included in the job, even though I'm pretty sure the advertisement quite clearly stated *room only, no board*.

I agree to eat his food if he allows me to cook dinner, and he doesn't put up much of a fight about that one. I'll be damned if I make him regret his decision to hire me.

During the day, I work my tail off doing all the jobs a regular, *male* farmhand would have done—maybe even more. At night I cook us dinner, and on my days off, I clean up around the house, unasked. I gain back the weight I lost in those sad days before I came here, some of it in pure muscle mass, the rest filling out my old curves.

For two months, Colt seems satisfied with my work, both outside the house and within. He even says so, with praise all the more sweet for its muttered reluctance, like, *You did all right out there today, Alex,* and, *This meatloaf reminds me of the one my mom used to make.*

But in the past few weeks, if possible, he seems even more reserved. He keeps his head bent during dinner and spends more time outside.

This worries me. I'm happy here, but I don't want to run him out of his own home.

Taking a brief break from my work refilling the feed troughs, I watch as he repairs the fence around the large corral, snipping and straightening the barbed wire.

His hands are ensconced in thick gloves, but I've seen over the past few days that inevitably some part of his skin—on his chin or his arm—will get snagged and bleed. This is what he's like, I realize. Wrapped in barbed wire to keep everyone out, but it must sting him, too.

I see that small pain sometimes, the stillness after each sharp cut. The loneliness of a single coffee mug laid out to dry. The hard look in his eye when he checked out my newly rounded ass just now. He longs for something, and it's the same thing I want, a little dirty and a lot rough.

He's a prime specimen of man, lean and large in all the right places. But the more I watch his impressive work ethic, his unassuming honor, the more I want the man inside. Only I don't see how that can happen. There's so much between us, layers of sharp and prickly metal wire, and I don't know how to get past it without cutting us both.

He returns to the house later and later each day, and though it's really none of my business, curiosity consumes me. What is he doing out there as I keep the pot roast warm in the oven? It's none of my business, but that doesn't stop me from walking to the stable where a light glows amber through the slatted doors.

I follow the sounds of gentle water in the side room that serves as both a tack room and a tool station. Standing in the doorway, I register only the sights I've seen before, albeit with furtive glances.

Colt stands at the utility sink, a wet rag pressed against the back of his neck. Water runs in darkening rivulets over bronzed shoulders and down his furred chest.

He's washing up, that's all. I should return to the house or call out so he's aware of my presence. Instead, I let my gaze slide along his now-slippery body, to where the water would soak into the waistband of his jeans.

But his waistband isn't where I thought it would be, buttoned up. Instead, the two sides of his fly splay open, and the damp-darkened white of his underwear is pushed down, allowing his curved cock to jut from his body. It's clearly quite hard, which he confirms by thrusting it into his fist.

He moans, a low sort of grumble, and my body responds with a strangled gasp. He looks up and—oh shit, he actually *looks up at me*, and I think I might melt onto the dusty floor, leaving nothing but a shameful wet spot where Alex used to be. That might be preferable to standing here, caught red-handed, having already made him so uncomfortable in his own home that he won't wank off there.

Though he doesn't look disturbed, as his nostrils flare, and he murmurs my name. He doesn't seem put off from the whole *wanking* business as his fist seems to tighten and—one, two—strokes his length.

I blink, but I really can't deny what is happening right now: he's masturbating while watching me.

He's pleasuring himself to the sight of me.

Lust is a strong current in my mind, but I force myself to still. I can turn around, away from the pretty muscles and the angry-aroused face of the most decent man I've ever met, and I would hate myself forever. Or I can go to him.

So I do, walking toward him on the heaviest feet known to man. I'm literally shaking, and I can't think why I'm so nervous. Except that I want this, badly. More than I had wanted a job and a place to live and food on the day I came here, I want this. To be connected to him with my body, my mind and whatever else there is knocking around inside us. Something meaningful, so that even if I had to drive away from Colt's farm tomorrow, the ripples of our joining would gently rock me in my sleep.

With my every step, his hand quickens, his lids lower. His lips part, and I'm sure he's going to come. He must be almost hurting himself, so tightly and so quickly. He releases a sound on every upstroke, like something that would come in the middle of a word, just *unhhhh*, breath expelled and body taut. He can't hold out anymore, I think. Any minute now, he'll climax, and it will be over.

I don't want it to be over. I want to watch this sight every night, like the sunset from the porch. More than that, I want to join in.

My knees hit the hard-packed dirt, bringing me eye to eye with the beautiful cock made blurry with motion and glistening with precum. I open my mouth, a little hesitantly. I want this, and I think he wants this, too. But I'm not sure. I need a sign. Just a hint that this is the right direction, that he doesn't think I'm overstepping the boundaries here.

"Your tits," he says on a groan. "Show me your tits."

That will work.

I look down at the slight swells of my breasts above the heather-gray camisole I'm wearing. When I'm working on the ranch, I wear a T-shirt or sometimes flannel, something sturdy to ward off the elements. But at night, I had recently begun stripping down before dinner. I'd felt more at home here, and so I began to dress more comfortably—more sparingly, too.

I wonder if that's why he's out here, pulling out a quick orgasm before joining me for dinner. Have I been teasing him without knowing in my comfy camisoles and soft, stretchy pants? More disturbing, have I known all along? Either way, it seems to have turned out all right. I pull the thin fabric over my head. My nipples pucker in the sweet night air.

I expect him to come at the sight of my tits, by request. Maybe he'll even come on me, spraying warm and wet onto the pale flesh. Instead, he slows his hand. In fact, it stops entirely, but his hips take up motion then, pushing into his fist. More leisurely now. As slow as he might actually fuck someone.

Dropping the wet rag into the sink behind him, he reaches out to touch my nipple. His finger is still cold and damp, and a shiver runs through me.

"So lovely," he says. "Do you want this? I don't know if I can even stop now, but I need to know if you—"

"Yes." *God, yes.*

"It wouldn't be right, if you didn't want to, if you thought you had to..."

I know what he means. He's worried I think I owe him sex in exchange for the housing and food and money he pays me. I'm not sure how to answer, because I do feel like I owe him. I *want* to owe him. My feelings of gratitude and relief are all tied up with other ones, tangled and roped with oh-so-ordinary things like lust and affection and maybe even love. They can't be separated out into neat little compartments. They're all how I feel for Colt, over full.

But I can't explain all this while I'm on my knees and he's

fucking his own fist right in front of me. So I do the next best thing; I reach for the head of his cock with my mouth. Though *reach* is too polite a word for what I really do. I lunge for it, but that's how I'm feeling now—hungry for him.

His taste is like a kaleidoscope on my tongue, salt and sweat and man, while my tongue swirls and swirls around him. I'm dizzy with lust, but he's there to ground me. He clamps on to the back of my head and holds me still, as still as his fist a minute ago, and pumps into me. I hear him groaning, those same low trebled noises that bounce around the hollow room and fill me up inside.

He moves faster and more roughly, exactly how I'd imagined it all those nights in the bedroom beside his. Except I had worried he'd be too careful, too gentle, but that was silly, I see now. He's the same with sex as with everything—hard and a little bit mean, but endearingly so, at least to me. I'm just a little perverse like that. In fact, I'd prefer for him to be rougher, to hold my hair and call me names, but I'm hopeful those things will come later. Like a kinky courting ritual, this slightly cruel blow job is just a portal to sweeter things.

I open my mouth and close my mind, letting myself become a vessel for him to use, trusting my body to him the way I've already entrusted my heart.

He doesn't disappoint, releasing thick cum into my mouth, which I swallow down eagerly. By the end, I'm panting and leaning my head against his leg while he pets my hair.

"You were so good, sweetheart. Did you like that?"

I murmur something unintelligible against the denim. I *loved* it, but I'm burning up inside, all fidgety and near to crying over it, and I don't know if it's finished now. There wasn't a section in the employee handbook titled "Unexpected Stable Sex with Your Cowboy Boss," or really a handbook at all, and with the receding of his lust, I'm suddenly self-conscious.

He rustles a bit. I think he must be tucking himself away in his jeans when I hear the zipper, but I face the ground. My cheeks feel hot with arousal and embarrassment and why won't he fuck me? Except I know the answer. I've already taken care of his fuck-urge, and now there's just me, horny and shamefully clinging to his leg.

He tugs me to standing and with careful but sure hands, takes off my jeans and my panties.

The surety in his touch eases some of my tension. He seems to have a plan, and thank god, because I want to follow it. He leads me over to a table that's strewn with tools and the bottom leather bits of a saddle. He clears it away and then pats the edge.

"Jump up here."

I stare at it. "I don't know. Will it break?" It's wide enough for me, and it's got all four legs, but I'm not sure how much trust I have in a random almost-outdoors table.

"It'll hold," he says. "I built it."

I built it. Which raises all sorts of questions. Did he expect to fuck a woman on this table when he built it? Or does he just include that specification in all his furniture-making plans—*must be fuck-sturdy*?

He gets impatient and lifts me by my waist.

Right as the flesh of my ass touches the cool wood, a worrisome thought flashes through my mind: *splinters.* But I don't even have to ask this time. I know the answer. He built it, and the surface feels smooth as butter against my ass.

He parts my legs with large, insistent palms and stares at me. Just stares at the place between my legs. My gut clenches. I know I've groomed there, but it's not the perfect smoothness I want for him. There aren't any Brazilian waxing salons in Paloma, and even if there were, I wouldn't really have spent the money. Stupid, stupid, why hadn't I done that?

"This is such a pretty pussy," he said, running two blunt fingers from bottom to top.

Ohhh, and without even knowing it, that's why. But there's more.

"I love how pink you are." He touches my nipples, tweaks them, one then the other. All the while, his other hand runs gently over swollen, slippery lips. "I love how ready you are to take me. So slick I could just slide right in."

"Do it," I breathe.

He pauses, then. "We have to talk first."

I let out a shuddery breath. He's the devil, the actual devil with horns on his head that I can't see. He's reduced me to this quivering mass of need and now he needs to handle it with all due haste. He needs to take out the renewed bulge I can see in his jeans and come inside me. If he doesn't, I'll just… I'll just…

My whole body trembles, on the cusp of a decision. Take or give. Leave or submit. Though I know what the answer will be; it's already decided. Even as I mentally brace against his steely delay, a small part of me revels in it. I love his selfishness to take his pleasure first and his control as he withholds mine. Maybe it's because I know with absolutely certainty that he'll take care of me. Or maybe it's because the glimmer in his eyes says he knows all of this is only making me hotter, bringing me higher. This is all for me as much as it's for him.

"What do we need to talk about?" I force myself to say.

"What do we need to talk about…*Sir*," he corrects.

"No," I say, although it's not really a refusal; it's surprise. Really? This is going to be an actual thing that we do? He'll give me orders, and I'll call him Sir? At the thought, a small bit of wetness tickles my opening, sliding onto his probing fingers. My face flushes.

He pauses, raising his hand between us, turning it this way and that, letting the moonlight reflect off my arousal. Then he puts his forefinger into his mouth and sucks.

My hips buck, so empty and cold without his touch. "Sir," I whisper. "Sir, Sir, Sir..." And I have no idea what I'm supposed to say after that. It doesn't even matter, because I've already said it all with the breathless litany. *Yes, anything, please, so much.*

"You need to promise that you aren't going to run off after this."

I'm dazed, but I try to focus. This seems important, and maybe the worst possible time to be having an important conversation. Or the best time. "Why...would I run off?"

"If you start worrying about our situation, with the job and the house, talk to me. If you're not getting what you need from me, ask me for it."

"Yes, of course."

His eyes narrowed. "I'm serious. I don't care why you ran before. It brought you here, after all. But you don't just cut out with a trunk full of boxes, not this time. If you get scared, you run *to* me, not away, understand?"

My breath hitches. I *had* been running, although not from anything in particular, just myself and my failures. My fears, which he seems to already know. He understands me; he accepts me—he wants me to stay. And I *will* be strong enough this time. At least, I want to be. I want to be solid and steady, like he is. I want to be next to him while I do it.

"Yes, Sir," I say quietly.

His gaze seems to bore into me before he relents, pressing a kiss on my lips. It deepens, and I part my lips. His hands are everywhere, my breasts, my back, holding me, securing me, and this is so much better than what I'd wanted before, the hard fucking.

At least until his lips descend in a languorous line—one kiss, two—dropping like breadcrumbs in a twist-turn path. His mouth closes over one nipple and tugs and worries and plays there until I'm crying or crying out, "Fuck me, oh please, oh Sir-Sir-Sir…"

And it's the very best thing ever, until the slippery silk of his tongue trails lower, down to where I'm pulsing and aching for him.

He's on the job, though. He's got it covered—with that clever tongue and those tender lips. He seems to know right where I ache, because he makes it worse before soothing it better.

I climb and come down at his command, bound by nothing more than the power I give him. I want and I plead and I think, *Maybe this time.* And then he flicks my clit, just once, and I think it must be now, oh god, now, now.

He chooses this moment to stand up straight, sending a wash of cool air to my clit, which feels like sleet against my damp, throbbing nub. I release a coarse groan of frustration that's not at all feminine, unless it's feminine to be demanding and ravenous for sex.

Though it might be, to him, because there's a half smile teasing lips made shimmery from my arousal. He likes me this way, groaning and desperate.

And well, that's convenient, because I am. Just like he said, I'm dying to be filled, and judging from the straining at his crotch and the way he absently rubs it, like assuaging an ache, he wants that, too.

He's the most single-mindedly industrious man I've ever met, so it figures that he'd apply that same intensity to sex. *Here's how we can more efficiently derive pleasure, with the swipe of my thumb on her clit. And look, when I lick her nipples, she shivers, yielding a higher touch per response ratio.*

"God," I say. "*God.*"

He raises one eyebrow. "What is it you want, Alex? If you need something, what are you supposed to do?"

He wants to appear detached, I know, but the tension lines around his mouth prove otherwise. What do I want? To get fucked, by him, and quickly. What am I supposed to do? Here I draw a blank, but I come up with an idea that my lust-fevered brain thinks is brilliant in its simplicity.

Beg.

"Please, Sir. Please fuck me. I need your thick cock so badly. So deeply. I'll squeeze you tight. I'll make it good for you."

He groans, loud and long, and it's not a regular sort of male sound, but instead animalistic and kind of scary. But my body responds with a jolt of recognition. We're not even people anymore, just sex animals, just conduits for feeling and fucking.

He flips me over, and I flail for a minute before latching my hands on to the other side of the worktable. I hear the small tear and slick sound of a condom being put on, and it freezes me for a second. He really *does* prepare for sex in all contingencies, even on a ranch with no other person for miles. Except me. And then the thought hits me. Did he *plan* for me to find him?

I'm distracted, though, when the wide, blunt head of his cock nudges into me from behind. It's hard to think when his hands smooth around my sides and cup my breasts. I can only gasp when he pulls me back, hard, dragging me onto him while he pushes from behind. We'd burn up from the friction if it weren't so wonderfully wet between us, sweat and sex coating our skin, turning our desperate scramble into a glide.

Despite the riotous sensations sparking through my body, I can't quite forget my worry. What's happening here, what does it mean? I gave him my heart before I'd even realized it was gone. And now my body's his, too, owned by him before he'd fully claimed it, surrendered before the demands were made. I had thought I had gotten stronger, but the clench in my heart feels painfully thin, like wet vellum held taut, and I want to ask him where we stand in the middle of a wild fucking—not good timing.

But he'd said to ask if I had a question, and he certainly hadn't shied away from the tough subjects even when my breasts were bared and my pussy open.

I push out a word on each thrust. "Are you… Do you want me?"

He slows but doesn't stop. I know the question sounds strange. His cock is thick and impossibly hard inside me right now. That's not an accident, like he tripped and plunged inside me to the hilt. Somehow his fist is tangled in my hair, while the fingertips of his other hand are held in questioning stillness around my nipple. These aren't the signs of a man disinterested.

So I hope he understands what I mean. There's only this breathless shorthand during sex, but it's an age-old question, really. Do you like me? Because I like you, love you, and if you don't feel that way back, this is all going to hurt much worse than the lip of the worktable where it juts into my hip—but I'd rather feel it now than later.

"From the first day I saw you," he says. "In every way, always."

I had thought if I found a way inside, there'd be no more pain. But even now that he's let me in, I feel the barbs that surround us. They sting and ache, sending chills along my skin. Even when he's sweet and lovely, it's a special kind of pain, heart hurt. It pricks at my eyes, and hot tears slide down my cheeks. But he doesn't stop.

He'll never stop, even when it hurts, because this is the price and the pleasure of loving a cowboy.

COWBOY ADONIS

Michael Bracken

N ude, he rose from the stock pond like a cowboy Adonis, his thick, uncut phallus not perceptibly affected by the cold water. With my high-end digital camera, I snapped off half a dozen photographs of the cowboy's wet, muscular body before he realized I was watching. He made no effort to turn away or cover himself but pushed dripping, shoulder-length black hair away from his face and said, "I thought I was alone out here."

"So did I."

I couldn't look away. The few men in my life had been pudgy, sun-deprived city boys exuding pretentiousness but not masculinity, nothing at all like the naked cowboy before me.

He took a T-shirt from the pile of clothes he'd stripped off before diving into the stock pond and pulled it on. The white cotton clung to his broad shoulders, thick chest and six-pack abdomen like a second skin. Then he settled a white Shantung straw Stetson on his head before reaching for his boxer-briefs. He pulled them on, pulled a tight-fitting pair of well-worn

Wranglers on over them, and then sat on the ground to put on his socks and Justin ropers.

After he pushed himself to his feet and brushed Texas from the seat of his Wranglers, he gave me a once-over, taking in finger-length blonde hair plastered to my head with sweat, a slender figure disguised by a loose-fitting University of Texas sweatshirt that masked my braless state, jeans so new I might have forgotten to take off all the tags, and hiking boots I wore to keep from twisting my ankles as I hiked across the rough, uneven pasture.

"What are you doing on my property?"

I'd entered the Bar-B-Dahl Ranch by hopping a gate a mile or so south from where we stood. "You're Mr. Dahl?"

"Mr. Dahl is my father," he said. "I'm Jason."

"I talked to your father, then," I explained. I introduced myself and told Jason about the magazine assignment I had, a rare opportunity to leave my Austin studio to take photographs of how the landscape had changed with the end of the drought. "Your father said it was okay as long as I didn't scare the cattle."

"You should have come up to the house and checked in," he said. "Someone needs to know you're here in case something happens."

"I'm okay," I said. "I have a cell phone."

He smirked. "Try it, Andrea."

I pulled out my iPhone and quickly realized I couldn't get a signal. As I returned it to my pocket, I asked, "So what could happen to me out here?"

"Rattlesnakes, scorpions and wild hogs," he said, listing just a few of the dangerous creatures I might encounter. Then he smiled and added, "And naked cowboys."

"I think I can handle the naked cowboys," I said, and the

thought of doing just that made my heat rise.

I must have blushed because Jason said, "You look like you're about to have a heatstroke. We should get you up to the house where you can cool off."

I glanced around. "How?"

A slight rise on the other side of the stock pond hid a battered, extended-cab dualie pickup truck, and soon we were inside the cab with the windows wide open because the truck lacked air-conditioning. The warm air assaulting us through the open windows quickly dried Jason's hair as the truck bucked along a rutted path toward the ranch house and away from the stock pond and the car I'd parked near the gate I'd hopped over.

"You don't get out of the city much, do you?" Jason asked over the sound of the engine.

"Why do you think that?"

"Designer jeans, pink hiking boots," he said as he reached behind my seat and felt around, "and no hat."

He tossed a sweat-stained gimme cap with the logo of a feed store embroidered on the front into my lap, and I put it on.

"Better?" I asked.

He took his eyes off the rutted path and looked me over. "It'll do."

The truck hit a bump that bounced me forward. I secured my camera with my right hand and braced myself against the truck's dashboard with my left. I saw Jason examining my hand and I held it up so he could see that I wore no jewelry. "No rings," I said, "if that's what you're looking for."

He smiled. "Be a pity to find a stray on our property and see that she carried another man's brand."

I snorted. The thought of any of the city boys I'd dated ever tying me down seemed preposterous.

"We don't get many women out here, Andrea, except for the

annual Cattlemen's Ball," Jason said, "and certainly none as pretty as you."

"You rope in many women with a line like that?"

"You'd be the first."

The truck hit another bump and I bounced across the seat toward Jason. He patted my knee and liquid fire shot through my entire body.

"You might want to fasten your seat belt before you get bucked out the window," he said. "I wouldn't want to lose you so soon."

I slid back to my side of the truck and strapped in. "What about you?" I asked. "You have anyone trying to corral you?"

"No, ma'am. I've been free range for quite a while now."

"Can't be tied down?"

He glanced at me. "I've been waiting for the right woman to walk into my life."

We crested a small rise and found the ranch house and outbuildings spread out before us. Jason brought the truck to a halt beside the house and led me inside.

A blast of air-conditioning hit me as I stepped through the door, sending an unexpected chill through my entire body that caused my nipples to dimple my sweatshirt. Being small-breasted and braless made my stiff nipples seem even more prominent as they pressed against the UT logo on my sweatshirt.

Jason noticed but said nothing as he led me into the living room of what was clearly a bachelor's residence and told me he shared the place with his father. He added, "But he's in Amarillo for the week."

I removed the gimme cap and unslung the camera strap from around my neck. As I placed the camera and cap on the coffee table next to a stack of *The Cattleman* magazines, Jason disappeared into the kitchen. He returned almost immediately with two cold bottles of Lone Star beer, both open.

He handed a bottle to me and downed much of his in one long pull. When he finished, Jason wiped his mouth with the back of his hand and regarded me thoughtfully. "You're still flushed."

"The heat," I lied. The ride in his truck had dried Jason but it had made me wet, wet in a way that no man had made me during the three years since I had opened my own studio.

Because I had spent that time looking at the world through my camera lens and not looking at it with my own two eyes, I had developed an extensive client list and a respectable income, but had allowed my personal life to grind to a complete halt. There wasn't a man in my life—not a lover, not a friend with benefits, not even a battery-operated substitute.

Now here I was, less than an arm's length away from a cowboy Adonis I had already seen naked, and I wanted him to take me in his arms.

I wanted him to take me.

I wanted him to—

"Is there something wrong with the beer?"

Shaken from my reverie, I asked, "Huh?"

"Your beer," Jason prompted. "You haven't even tasted it."

I took a quick swig. "It's fine."

"Your color is a little better."

"So, your father's in Amarillo," I said, changing the subject. "Anyone else here?"

"It's just us."

"Just us," I repeated as I stared into his eyes. I wet my lips with the tip of my tongue and wished I'd had the foresight to wear lipstick. "Alone. Just you and me."

Somehow Jason understood the incoherent message I was sending him. He put his hands on my hips and pulled me close.

He stared deep into my eyes for a moment, as if waiting for me to stop him. Softly, almost in a whisper, he said, "You can use your cell phone now if you think you've encountered something dangerous."

"Like a rattlesnake or a scorpion or a wild hog?"

He smiled. "Or a naked cowboy."

I arched an eyebrow. "You're not naked yet."

He removed his Stetson and placed it on my head. Then he pressed his lips against mine, and we kissed. The first kiss was slow with our mouths closed. The second was deeper, lasted longer. I could feel his cock stirring within his Wranglers and pressing against my pubic mound through the thick denim of our jeans.

His work-hardened hands slid up under my sweatshirt until the balls of his thumbs pressed against my erect nipples.

Without prompting, I lifted my arms and he pushed my UT sweatshirt up and off, revealing my small breasts and turgid nipples. He tossed the sweatshirt aside and dropped to his knees in front of me. After unfastening my jeans, he hooked his thumbs in the waistband of my panties and pulled my pants and underwear to my knees. They slid the rest of the way to my ankles as Jason's warm breath tickled the triangular patch of blonde hair at the juncture of my thighs.

He grabbed my asscheeks, pulled my pubic mound tight against his face and covered my pussy with his mouth. He licked the length of my slick slit, tasting my desire before he parted my labia with his tongue and teased the swollen bud of my clit. His five o'clock shadow sandpapered the insides of my thighs as he tongued me, and before long I couldn't restrain myself.

My legs buckled as an orgasm erupted within me.

Jason caught me as I collapsed. He carried me through the sprawling ranch house to his bedroom, his Stetson falling to the floor somewhere along the way. He threw me across his king-sized bed and pulled off the last of my clothing.

Then he stripped off his clothes, revealing what I had already seen and admired, and climbed onto the bed to kneel between my widespread thighs. His cock stood firm and erect, and I took it in both hands. I pulled the foreskin away from the swollen purple head and wiped away a glistening drop of precum with the ball of my thumb before guiding him toward my cunt.

He entered me slowly at first, but once he was certain I was well lubricated with desire, he slammed his cock all the way into me. As he drew back and did it a second time, I wrapped my legs around his waist and hooked my ankles together behind the small of his back. Then I wrapped my hands around his neck and pulled his face down to mine.

We kissed deep and hard. The taste of my arousal on his lips and tongue excited me even more, and I drove my hips upward to meet every one of Jason's powerful thrusts. He rode me hard and fast. No man had ever taken me this way, so confidently, so powerfully, so aggressively, and I responded in the only way I could.

I came and came hard.

I wanted Jason to stop, but I thought I'd die if he didn't continue.

I tilted my head back and screamed.

And he slammed into me one last time before he came.

He collapsed atop me, his thick penis continuing to spasm inside me as my pussy clenched and released around it as if attempting to milk him dry.

Afterward—after we had caught our breath and I lay wrapped in his arms—he asked, "Did you get all the photographs you need?"

"No," I told him. "I was interrupted."

"I can show you around the ranch tomorrow," he said, "if you wish."

"We'll need to retrieve my car tonight."

"We can do that," Jason said as he guided my hand to his thickening arousal, "but not right away."

We made love a second time, slower but with no less intensity, then retrieved my car. I spent the night in Jason's bed. The next day he escorted me around the ranch, stopping the truck whenever I saw something I wanted to photograph.

We made love one last time late that evening before I returned to Austin. I completed the assignment a few days after I returned home and mailed Jason a copy of the magazine when it was published two months later.

But the best photographs I'd taken on assignment weren't the ones in the magazine; they were the photographs I'd taken of Jason rising nude from the stock pond. I made a print of the best one and hung it in my bedroom so that I could see my cowboy Adonis every night before I fell asleep and every morning when I awoke, and I hung the sweat-stained gimme cap next to it.

Now that I'd had a cowboy, no city boy would ever be man enough for me, and I vowed to return to the Bar-B-Dahl Ranch where I knew Jason was awaiting my return.

He'd even promised to take me swimming in the stock pond.

DENIM
AND LACE

Robie Madison

Your handsome-as-sin cowboy is staring at you again."

Luella Jean's deadpan drawl was barely audible above the raucous noise inside the Hold 'Em Tight Saloon, but Margot Goodwin heard her cousin just fine, thank you, as the band struck up yet another depressing love 'em and lose 'em Country and Western song.

Margot took a slug straight from her beer bottle in the desperate hope it might numb her senses. Which she'd apparently lost the moment she'd stepped onto Texas soil. The offer of a free beer at the bar her cousin worked at wasn't worth being subjected to a night of torturous tunes about love gone wrong.

"He's not my cowboy," she said, because if he liked this music he was definitely not the man for her. Whatever happened to the idea of love gone right?

"Yet," Luella Jean murmured. "But I think that's about to change."

And Margot couldn't help herself. She stole a glance past her cousin's shoulder into the mirror behind the bar. She didn't have to ask which cowboy Luella Jean thought was hers. He was already on his feet, scrubbing his hands across his jeans and, with one last look at his friends, sauntering toward her.

Even Margot, down on men as she was, had to admit he was quite a specimen. Topping six feet, his sandy hair could have used a cut, and he was way too young. Feeling all of her twenty-seven years, she downed another mouthful of beer—a beverage she was fairly certain the *boy* heading toward her wasn't legally allowed to imbibe.

"Don't you have thirsty customers to serve?" she asked when Luella Jean stood there with a front row seat for the coming show.

Her cousin made a pretense of wiping down the bar with the cloth in her hand. "Play nice now, you hear?" she said and was gone.

Margot drew a deep, calming breath. He was going to ask her to dance, and Margot had her answer all planned out. A polite, but firm, no thanks.

She wasn't prepared for his voice, deep, full of Southern comfort—and confidence. She'd give him that. He held out his hand in invitation. It was large and calloused and without really knowing why, she hesitated.

Uh-huh, like she could fool herself. From his size-extra-big cowboy boots on up, he was a long, lean temptation in denim, pure and simple.

Still, that was no excuse to rob the cradle, even if she did appreciate all those gorgeously sculpted muscles just begging to be caressed beneath the washed-out blue. Then she made the mistake of looking at his face. His eyes were a really warm shade of brown and filled with the certainty she was going to turn him down.

She tipped the beer bottle back for one last drink and from beneath her eyelashes she watched as his gaze slid down her exposed throat to the cluster of silver hearts hanging from a chain around her neck.

The fact he actually smiled, and that he didn't glance any lower, decided his fate. She plunked the bottle onto the bar and set her hand in his.

What was the harm in indulging in one flirtation-filled dance with a hot, young stud? A tendril of heat skittered along her arm as she allowed him to pull her onto the dance floor.

The song changed to something more up-tempo, and she lost herself in the music and the moves.

The cowboy could dance; she'd give him that, too. Then he swung her out and twirled her around once, twice, three times before tugging her just hard enough that she smacked against his deliciously solid torso when he reeled her in. The muscles in his arm shifted and tightened as he slid it round her waist, crushing her to his chest, surrounding her with his masculine heat. A sizable erection nudged her belly.

Whoa, there cowboy. Her breath caught. They'd finished their dance, but it seemed he wasn't willing to let her go just yet.

"I take it you're happy to see me," she said, teasing him just a little because she hadn't pushed away from his embrace. His hold was sturdy and oddly protective given all the electrical impulses zinging between them.

A blush stained his face, but he looked her in the eye. "Yes, ma'am."

At that she had to laugh. "Seriously, you're calling a woman you have a hard-on for ma'am?"

"Yes, ma—" He shut his mouth and nodded.

"Maggie," she said, which wasn't exactly a lie, but an old

nickname. "Maggie Smith." And, okay, that last part was a total fabrication.

"Ben," he said and glanced past her head at his cowboy buddies still sitting around the table before he looked at her again.

For a long moment, he just stood there looking and swaying. Not even bothering to dance anymore, which actually showed some taste since the band was playing another melancholy melody. But beneath her hand, his heart hammered double-time against his rib cage.

She licked her lips, suddenly parched. When his gaze tracked the movement, her heart kicked up a notch.

Uh-huh, like her heart racing at Indianapolis 500 speeds had nothing to do with the lazy path his fingers were making up and down her side, turning her core to molten lava. God, one dance and a few caresses and her panties were already soaked.

"Maggie."

She blinked up through a decidedly sensual fog and smiled.

If anything the flush deepened along his cheeks. To hide his embarrassment, he bent his head and nuzzled her hair. He swore a soft "Damn it all, anyway," but then he lifted his head, took another quick glance at his friends and then down at her.

He cleared his throat. "I can't afford you, but I gotta ask."

Whoa, cowboy. Margot's eyebrows shot up. He thought she was hooker?

She tried to grab hold of her common sense, but got a fistful of buttery, soft shirt instead, which maybe explained why she wasn't so much offended as curious. For details. From a purely academic point of view, of course.

"Just how old are you?" she asked.

"Twenty," he said, then paused and added, "next month."

Fact one, he was nineteen. Fact two—

"Just how much can you afford?"

"A hundred bucks," he said grimacing as though the amount might be a giant insult.

Well, the good news was, if she took the job she could buy that new pair of jeans she had her eye on. Only there was the little matter of fact number three. The small fortune she'd spent acquiring two degrees in mathematics attested to her aptitude with numbers, and frankly something didn't add up. What horny, nineteen-year-old cowboy, especially a tall, good-looking one, paid for sex?

"And how did you and your friends figure out I was, ah, looking to make a hundred bucks tonight?"

It had to be the shirt. Luella Jean had insisted Margot borrow one of hers, to be authentic and all, but then her cousin didn't have a size-C cup. A substantial amount of black lace was on display because the damn thing barely buttoned up past her naval.

"Your shoes," he said. "They're real—I like them. A lot, but Shane said they meant you were a high class—" He cleared his throat. "He said you were way out of my league and that I couldn't afford a dance let alone a...a... Shane called them—"

"Fuck-me heels," she said, catching on real fast, though she wasn't sure if three inches qualified. She didn't like to go much higher. As it was, wearing them she was five-ten to his six-two, which was why he couldn't hide the fact he turned redder than a tomato when he hesitated over saying the *H* word or the *F* word.

But height requirements aside, she had to admit her shoes definitely screamed sex appeal. Cream peep toes, with rhinestones studding the sole that ran up the arch of her foot and the outside length of the heel.

So yeah, she caught on and immediately realized question period was over. She had to tell him the truth. "Ben."

His face was buried in her hair again. "Yeah."

"It's a very nice offer, but I'm not a hooker. My cousin is the bartender, and I just came in for a drink and a visit."

He groaned. "Jesus, Clay's gonna kill me."

He sounded downright miserable and started to pull away, likely mortified his so-called friends had twisted his romantic notions about her fantasy-inducing footwear into something so wrong. He glanced up, looking for his friends, but she'd shuffled them in a semicircle, out of the line of sight of their table.

She slid her hand up his chest and curled her fingers around the back of his neck. "Did I say you could move?"

He stilled, and for a tiny moment she wondered if she'd read him wrong.

"No, ma'am—Maggie."

"I take it Clay isn't one of your friends at the table."

He shook his head. "I met them on the circuit."

In other words, they weren't his friends at all.

"So you put down a hundred dollars," she said, stood on her tiptoes and pulled his head down. "And what were you hoping I would do for that kind of money, Ben?"

He shuddered. His hand slipped down to cup her ass, and he notched his denim-clad cock hard against her pussy. His breath hitched. Or maybe it was hers, she couldn't be sure.

"Anything I could get," he whispered in that low Southern drawl of his. "Just as long as you wear those shoes."

"And how much did Shane bet?"

He flinched, but he learned fast and didn't pull away. He didn't immediately answer either.

"How much, Ben?" She dropped her voice, making it clear it was a command.

"Ten bucks, which I won 'cause you danced with me, but that means I lost ninety."

And finally the numbers added up to an equation she didn't like at all. Shane was quite the scam artist.

"I don't think so," she said softly.

"But you're not a—"

"Is that a 'no thank you, ma'am' to allowing me to have my way with you?" she asked, giving him a steady stare to make the invitation as clear as she could.

"No. I mean, yes ma'am, Maggie," he said, stumbling over the words. "Please."

He might be young and naïve, but he was legal, willing and he loved her shoes. Besides, she was now all hot and bothered by erotic images of him kneeling in front of her—minus all that denim.

For the second time that night, heat scorched her nerve endings. All Ben did was settle his hand along the small of her back to usher her into his sleeper trailer. But she was well aware the neat, intimate space was a window into his life as a cowboy on the rodeo circuit, while she'd revealed almost nothing about her own.

They'd left the saloon in her vehicle—her cousin's truck, actually—and she'd insisted they go to his place, because that way she had an exit strategy, because she still wasn't quite sure what she'd signed up for.

Against her hair, he whispered her name—or at least the one she'd given him. The word cascaded over her, drenching her skin with sinful expectations. His. Definitely hers.

She sucked in a breath, caught her bottom lip between her teeth to bite back a moan, but it did no good. He nipped her earlobe, like a playful cub, only there was no mistaking his intent when his huge, hard erection pressed firmly against her backside.

It wasn't easy, but she did step away from all that delectable male heat and turned to face him. Business before pleasure. She reached for the roll of bills tucked into her cleavage. It had seemed like the kind of place a hooker would stash her cash. Shane and his friends hadn't been too happy seeing it disappear inside so inaccessible a place.

"Ma'am, Maggie, don't."

They both knew it was his money, so she didn't bother debating the issue. She had a pretty good idea why he'd stopped her. The atmosphere inside the tiny living space was redolent with arousal. His. Definitely hers.

A turbulent storm threatened to swamp her with sensual stimulation. She'd never had trouble asking for what she wanted—or giving as good as she got. But she hadn't had much—well, any—experience with the whole dominatrix scenario.

The only things she knew for certain were that Ben got as excited as a puppy when she took charge, and that the mere thought of dominating the handsome young man elicited an erotic excitement she hadn't experienced in a long time.

She took a quick glance around, spotted a slim slab of countertop and took a step toward it. A second later, she hoisted herself onto her perch, ready to fulfil his fantasy—if she could.

Crooking a finger, she signaled that he should come closer. She judged the distance between them with precision, stuck her leg out, and planted the sole of her peep toe along the solid length of his shaft. "That's far enough."

Ben's gaze dropped to her foot. His breathing turned shallow—short, desperate pants of air that echoed around the compact room.

She pulled the bills from her bra and fanned them out for him to see. "You want your money back, you have to earn it."

He traced the path of rhinestones trailing down the heel

with his index finger and gave her a lazy, wicked smile. "Yes, ma'—"

The door of the trailer crashed open.

Margot jumped. She hit the edge of the counter on the way down, and with a total lack of grace and poise, would have fallen flat on her butt if Ben hadn't caught her. She clung to him and blinked, trying to take in the dark, hulking presence filling the small doorway.

"What the—" a voice boomed.

"Hi, Clay," Ben said.

Clay took a step forward.

Margot's jaw dropped. Six feet of stunningly virile male stomped closer. Wide shoulders filled out a plain black T-shirt to perfection. A pair of jeans accentuated lean hips and sinewy thighs, proving there wasn't an ounce of anything except muscle on this man's well-built frame. His slightly battered face suggested he'd honed his powerful body by taking life head on.

And this moment was no exception. His gaze was a brazen strip search down the length of her body. And she was a fool if she thought she could hide her reaction. Already mildly aroused, her breasts ached, the tips jutting against the thin layers of lace and cotton. The folds of her pussy quivered with the need to be filled by a hard, hot length of cock. She wouldn't have been surprised if his nostrils had flared to catch her scent, so dark and feral was the glance he gave her.

"I couldn't find you at the saloon, but I heard quite a story from Shane." He was talking to Ben, but he hadn't taken his eyes off her. "Made me wonder if you'd been kicked by one too many bucking broncos, boy. I promised your mama I'd look out for you."

Ben's arms tightened around her. "I haven't been kicked by any broncos."

Ben's belligerent tone was halfhearted. And she guessed he was thinking, if not for her, it had been a close call. The skeptical look on Clay's face suggested he could guess how close without being told any details.

"Yet," Clay said with a certainty about the hand life dealt a man on the rodeo circuit. "So that wad of money in the lady's hand belongs to..."

"It's mine," Ben said at the same time she said, "His."

She straightened away from Ben and put the pile of bills on the counter. She recognized a lose 'em situation when she saw one.

"Well, thanks Ben—" she said at the same time Clay said, "Aren't you going to introduce us, Ben?"

Her gaze shot to Clay.

"She says her name's Maggie Smith," Ben said surprising the hell out of her, because his tone said he didn't believe her.

She promptly closed her gaping mouth, but not before she caught Clay suppressing a grin. She glanced up at Ben who shrugged as if his observation was no big deal. "I figured you were being safe and that it was a—"

"Nickname," she said. "Well, the Maggie part is. My name's Margot."

"Hi Margot, I'm Clay," Clay said, drawing her attention again.

"I figured that out," she said and wondered what was going on with all the introductions when she was about to leave. "Well, I'd better be—"

"And once you, ah, settled with Shane," Clay said talking right over her. "You brought Margot home because..."

As expected, Ben blushed and refused to meet Clay's eyes.

Margot wrinkled her nose. "I believe it's my fuck-me shoes that, ah, got me the invite," she said because Clay seemed to expect an answer.

His gaze dropped to her feet. One brow arched. "Aren't they a little short?"

"They've got rhinestones, Clay," Ben said, then pressed his lips together.

She obligingly twisted her ankle to show off the sparkles on the sole and heel.

"I see that," Clay said. "So what? You planned to make love to the woman's shoes?"

His voice was a mix of gentle teasing and curiosity, and she got the distinct impression Ben and Clay had been down this road before.

Ben didn't seem to mind. Although blushing, he wore that wicked sexy smile of his again. "She has to be wearing them," he said. "And we were—"

"Yeah, I got an eyeful of just what you were doing when I walked in the door."

Ben's unrepentant grin widened.

"Um, excuse me," she said. "I'm standing right here, and we weren't doing anything." Much.

Big mistake inserting herself into the conversation.

Clay sauntered towards her. "So I'm totally misinformed, even though I'm positive I saw your fuck-me shoe planted on Ben's cock."

"Yeah, you positively saw that," Ben said, which was no help whatsoever.

"Margot?"

It took her a minute to realize Clay was waiting for her answer. Maybe because he was now standing right in front of her, blocking her view of the way out.

"What Ben said," she said. And felt the slow burn of a blush sweep up her face.

"So, just to get my facts straight," Clay said as calmly as if they were discussing the weather. "At some point before, during or after your admiration of her footwear, you did actually plan to fuck Margot, right?"

Margot's jaw sagged. He didn't have to be a dick about it.

He took a step closer, invading her personal space and every one of her senses. Her pheromones began working over-time coping with the high-T atmosphere swirling around her. And the only coherent thought she had was, *I want some now.* Fortunately, her brain was too slow sending the message to her mouth, so she didn't say the words out loud.

"Sweetheart, I could smell your sweet heat from the doorway."

What? Forget coherent brain function. Quite possibly her autonomic nervous system just short circuited. She didn't seem able to breathe.

"And I want some," he said.

"Maggie likes it when you say please, Clay."

"Please."

The word was barely a whisper across her skin, but it seared her just the same.

She looked at Clay. Really looked at him. His eyes sparked with lust like thunderbolts across an afternoon sky. And then she looked at Ben, who didn't seem the least bit upset at the idea of having to share her.

Share. Her. As in, she hadn't lost them at all.

Clay stepped to one side. "Are you in?"

And she realized Clay no longer blocked the path to the door. He'd made his request, and she could either accept or not. She could leave if she wanted, and they'd let her go.

"Please, ma'am," Ben said.

Margot looked from Clay's hard, still features to Ben's puppy dog eyes. What the hell? It was obvious that one him plus one her plus another him was a highly combustible combination. "I'm in," she said. "As long as I get to keep my shoes on."

"She's trying to get into my pants again," Ben said.

Yes, well, he'd already stripped off her jeans and it wasn't fair. He and Clay had one woman to undress, while she had two men in way too many clothes and not nearly enough skin.

Clay chuckled. His breath tickled the back of her neck, sending a shiver of need down her spine. "I'll distract her while you find a solution."

Distract her. He'd begun distracting her about a second after she'd caved to his request. About the only reasoned thought she'd had since was *more*. Sometimes, like a moment ago, she wanted more scrumptious male flesh exposed for her pleasure. She was greedy for another taste, another touch. Of Ben's smooth, lean muscles and the smattering of fine hair down the center of his chest. Of Clay's rougher, battle-scarred skin covered in dark fur.

She bit her lip as the tip of Clay's tongue traced a path down the side of her neck to her collarbone. She swallowed the guttural sound of longing that threatened to escape, because sometimes, like right now, she wanted to scream.

The men wanted to explore every square inch of her. And she wanted that too. God, she truly did. But they were so damn slow and the tsunami was building out of control inside her, and there wasn't a thing she could do to stop it.

"Here, try this," Ben said.

She frowned because he was holding up the length of silk scarf she used as a belt.

"Yep, that'll do," Clay said.

"Do for what?" she asked.

Ben just grinned. "You're interfering with my fun, and Clay's a champion tie-down roper."

She fought. "But I want…"

"Shh, now," Clay said, pinning her hands behind her back with ease. "It's our turn to worry about providing what you want."

She shook her head, but it was impossible to argue. He threaded the silken tie between her wrists and around her arms in some intricately seductive pattern that left her hands cupped behind her. And then he stepped forward into the small void between them.

His large, denim-clad erection filled her palms. He stilled behind her, as if waiting to see if she'd accept him. She had to concentrate against the assault to her senses, but somehow she sent the right signals to her fingers, and they squeezed the hard length.

A soft growl rumbled past his throat. He ground his cock against her, and she sank against him in surrender, his coarse chest hair rasping against the sensitive skin of her back.

That seemed to be the signal Ben needed. He slid to his knees in front of her and she dimly remembered this was the fantasy she'd envisioned. Only in her version he wasn't still wearing his jeans.

"She's soaking wet, Clay," he said, a finger stroking her slit through her underwear.

"I know," she said. "Now do something about it."

Clay's hands slid around her waist, stilling her impatient demands for attention. His fingers skimmed the edge of her panties. "On or off."

She whimpered at the needless delay.

"The lace is pretty," Ben said. "But I want to taste her."

Margot watched, mesmerized as they stripped her bare. And then Ben's mouth was on her. Hot, hungry. He licked her pussy, eagerly lapping the juices. His tongue delved deeper into her folds, impatiently searching for more.

She was battered by an erotic storm raging around her, through her. Caught between the one man's devastatingly wicked tongue-fuck of her bare pussy and the other man's denim-clad cock dry-fucking her hands.

"Let go," a voice rumbled in her ear.

She hovered on the edge, alternately begging and ordering Ben and Clay to take her the rest of the way. And then her neck arched and she screamed, wanton and uncaring who heard her, giving a keening wail as wildfire blazed across her skin. She thought she heard Ben cry out, but she was too far gone to care.

It took Margot a moment to realize her arms were free, that she was being held in Clay's arms, and that he still had his pants on while she was bare-ass naked.

"Where's Ben?" she asked, too dazed to look for herself.

Clay turned and nodded toward the couch.

"He fell asleep."

"But he didn't. Did he?" She was a little confused about the details.

"Let's just say he's going to have to throw those jeans in the laundry tomorrow."

"Oh," she said. "Where are you taking me?"

"Somewhere private."

She'd thought the trailer was one big room, but she quickly discovered there was a small bedroom behind a curtain. A bedroom with a queen-sized bed taking up most of the space.

Clay knelt on the edge of the mattress and lowered her reverently onto the bedspread. His hand skimmed the length of her leg to her foot.

"Permission to lose the shoes," he said in a tone that didn't sound as though he was really asking.

She nodded.

The heels hit the floor and he crawled up beside her.

"I take it you're happy to see me," she said.

He laughed. "Yeah," he said, tracing lazy patterns across her skin. "I'm an old man. I'm going to need a lot more time."

She smiled. "Just how old are you?"

"Thirty," he said. Paused and added, "next year."

"You need to lose the pants," she said.

"Does that mean you'll stay?"

Less than a minute later a pile of denim joined her shoes on the floor, and they both had her answer.

ONE-TRACK COWBOY

Delilah Devlin

With our horses' reins tied to tree branches, we stood by their heads soothing them as a helicopter's blades whipped up dust from above. While the bird lifted the hikers in baskets, one at a time, relief that we'd found the teenagers alive, if hungry, warred with my disappointment the journey was nearly over.

Once the second basket was safely aboard, Zane Red Elk looked over his shoulder at me. As always, his stoic expression was impossible to read. "Want me to signal them to send the basket down to pick you up too?" he asked, voice dead even.

I wondered why he asked. He could simply radio the request; his job was done. If I refused, he'd be stuck getting me back to the park headquarters, two days—and nights—away.

I hesitated. Was he offering me an option because he felt it was polite or because he hoped I'd stay? Maybe he read the reason for my indecision as easily as he had the tracks the boys' sneakers left in hard rock and sifting dirt. He lifted the radio and told the helicopter to head back to civilization and the waiting ambulance.

I stood atop a bare ridge, my face no doubt reflecting every bit of yearning I felt. The emotion hit me squarely in the belly. As hard as the tracker had been on me, I wasn't ready to leave him.

The last two days had been a revelation. I'd been working for the park service for three years, and it was the first time I'd been selected to participate in a search for missing hikers. When the boys failed to return to their vehicle and hadn't talked to relatives in days, we'd feared the worst. A search was organized involving volunteers and members of the park service, local law enforcement and Texas Rangers, and was conducted from the ground and the air.

Zane was enlisted due to his tracking expertise and his intimate knowledge of the area. When he wasn't busy with his nearby horse ranch, he led photographers and hunters through the canyon.

We rode two of his personal horses—Zane on a tall black gelding and me on an even-tempered bay mare. After two days in the saddle, despite the fact I rode often for relaxation, my ass was numb.

Zane flicked a glance my way, turned off the radio and stowed it in his gear. There'd be no need to keep in contact with the team now that the search was over. We'd head back the way we came. I hoped he'd take his time.

I wanted time to savor the silence and my growing attraction to the stone-faced Comanche cowboy who'd begun this journey more than a little irritated I'd insisted on accompanying him. I guess he'd thought I wouldn't be able to keep up. I'd earned his grudging admiration the first time we'd taken our horses down an arroyo and I hadn't freaked at the steep decline. I'd cemented his respect the first night we'd stopped and set up camp. With a quiet efficiency that matched his, I'd cared for my horse and then set about sweeping away brush and rolling out my sleeping bag, never complaining about the lack of a crackling fire to provide comfort in the darkness.

For two days, we'd barely spoken, except when he'd paused to point out the signs he'd found—broken branches, boot scuffs, dried puddles where the two young boys urinated against a tree or behind a boulder.

I trusted his instincts. Not something I did easily. He was so competent and briskly impatient that I'd gone along with his every suggestion, biting my tongue before adding my own two cents. He didn't need them.

And now we'd be alone. Miles and miles from civilization. For the first time since I'd begun this journey, anticipation rather than quiet dread thrummed in my chest.

If he felt it too, he hid it well. He repacked his gear, ran his hands over his horse's head and flanks, then lifted his hooves to check his shoes. I followed suit, not wanting to earn his disgust if my horse fell lame because I'd been too moon-eyed to see to the mare's welfare first.

When I dropped the last hoof to the ground, I straightened. Zane stood closer than I expected. I drew back startled, my eyes widening. His face hovered over mine, so still, his dark eyes watchful, that my breath caught and held. What was he searching for?

I went with my gut, with my own desire. My lips parted as I let my head fall back. An invitation extended with the lowering of my eyelids. Beneath the sweep of my lashes, I noted the tensing of his jaw, the narrowing of his gaze. He was looking at my mouth.

And then slowly, he bent closer, his mouth drawing nearer.

"We should head back into the canyon and follow the edge of the stream."

I drew in a ragged breath. He was so damn close. *Just kiss me.*

He moved away, but not before I saw one corner of his firm mouth twitch.

My face grew hot. Almost as hot as the juncture of my thighs where moisture pooled. Only once before, when he'd checked my seat on his horse and the length of my stirrups before we left the parking lot, had he stood that near. And then, his hand had been on my boot, easing it in and out of my stirrups, adjusting the length a notch. His hand had brushed my calf just above my boot, but I'd assumed it was accidental, because he certainly hadn't given me any clear sign he was as aware of my body as I was of his.

From that first moment when he'd arrived in his big Ford pickup with an old dented trailer in tow, I'd been intensely aware of him. I was to lead a ground team up one possible trailhead while another team followed a well-established hiking route. We'd all stood staring at the park map behind the Plexiglas; Zane beside my shoulder as I'd traced the first team's route with a finger.

Zane had shaken his head. "Do we even know that was where they planned to go?"

The trail was popular. "Where would you go?"

"Straight up the ridge overlooking the canyon."

The face of the bare outcropping of rock was a favorite with climbers, but the rugged trail along its edge led into wild back-country. Only skilled hikers, and ones who carried proper gear, including GPS and radios, should ever attempt it.

The two boys didn't have the extra gear and carried only sleeping bags and light packs with food for two days. Their parents had thought they intended to sleep in the canyon camping area, but the ranger at the station remembered them standing in front of this very map and asking about trails.

Zane and I took the harder route. The one he said two boys who liked to look for trouble would go. By the end of day one, we'd found signs.

Zane bent over his saddle, peering at the dusty trail. "Two hikers."

"We don't know it's our boys."

"It's two men. Wide strides. Light steps. They don't weigh much. And they're heading straight up. They haven't stopped to eat. There's no trash. My guess is they wanted to make the first bluff and camp there for the night to watch the sunset."

On horseback, we'd made the bluff before noon. The boys' campsite was evident from the trash they'd only half buried. Ramen bags. Energy bar wrappers.

Zane and I hadn't stopped until we'd found their second campsite. One they'd taken even less time to clean up, because it was obvious they were already scared. They'd traveled in nearly a circle before bedding down, footsteps crossing their own paths.

With darkness falling, we'd stopped to rest the horses and rolled out our sleeping bags. The Army MRE bags we carried had provided a hot meal with a huge number of calories. I hadn't wanted to finish mine, but he'd pushed the crackers and peanut butter at me, silently insisting I eat everything. I'd guessed he didn't want me lagging from lack of energy or complaining of hunger.

We'd lain on the dirt, three feet between our bags, beneath a starry sky. And although my body was tired and aching, I'd been too aware of his proximity to fall asleep quickly. I kept remembering how he'd looked that day, straw cowboy hat atop his dark hair, his long black braid swaying between his shoulders. He wore a light chambray, long-sleeved shirt over a dark tee. His jeans were Wranglers that hugged his hard ass and thick thighs. Zane was tall, and from the light scruff of beard on his jaw, not full-blooded Native American, although his sharp, wide cheekbones and tawny skin bespoke the majority of his heritage.

Even now, my horse needing barely a nudge to follow Zane happily down a ravine, my gaze rested on his tall, lean frame. Without the dreadful urgency that had filled me while we'd searched, my thoughts were now consumed by my partner.

I didn't know a thing about his personal life. He didn't wear a ring, but what did that signify? And what had that "moment" back there on the ridgeline been about? Was he mocking me because he knew I was attracted? Or was he interested too?

And if he wanted me, was it because I was the only female for miles in this wilderness? I hoped like hell not. I hadn't been with a man in a long while, and I didn't think I could handle something as shallow as a convenience fuck.

If fucking was even something on his mind, I couldn't tell. He didn't glance back. Not once. If he was interested in *me*, wouldn't he be as curious as me and slyly watchful?

We followed a dry creek bed with a gradual decline toward the river bisecting the park. As it was early summer, the water was still high against the banks. Inviting. My horse was certainly eager. I let her have her head, and she trotted toward the edge of the water. I dismounted, dropped her reins and let her step into the water, her head ducking to snuffle and drink.

The chink of metal and dull thud of leather hitting the ground sparked my interest, and I came around my horse, watching as Zane tossed his saddle beside the packs already on the ground.

"I take it we'll be here for a while."

"We've pushed the horses hard."

He didn't give any more of an explanation, but I read the challenge in his gaze. I nodded slowly and turned back to my horse, following his example to relieve my mare of her burden.

When I loosened the cinch around her abdomen, the saddle lifted away unexpectedly. Zane hadn't helped me with my gear since we'd started. Now the simple action turned me on more than a hot glance might have. His body was tight. His movements a little less graceful than usual. When he set down the saddle and straightened, I could see why. The bulge that lay trapped against his thigh was unmistakable.

My mouth went dry. "Think the water's cold?" I asked, inanely. The water was certainly cooler than the air. But, I needed to say something other than: "I hope that erection's for me."

I did my best to keep my gaze on his face, but couldn't help flitting down to check out his impressive hard-on. I felt as gauche as a teenager.

"Bathe," he said quietly, then turned and began to strip.

I liked his economy of movement. The unfussy way he tugged and pulled and quickly dropped his clothes in a heap beside his feet.

I admired his nakedness, the round firmness of his backside, the ropey muscles framing his spine. When he reached behind him for his ponytail and began to sift the braid free, my mouth pooled with saliva. His hair was black and shining blue where the sun hit it. Thick. My fingers curled at my sides.

And then he turned, his gaze raking over me. His mouth tightened. Was that annoyance? I noted his expression, only fleetingly, because my gaze dropped straight to his cock, which was extended, the blunt cap glistening with a hint of moisture. It was long and thick, the shaft straight and rising from a dark, sparse thatch of hair.

"Do you need help?" he asked, voice silky like I'd never heard it before.

A quiver shook my belly, making my knees weak, and I knew if I tried to take off my boots standing, I'd fall on my face. I didn't answer, simply waited as he narrowed his eyes and strode toward me, his height and masculine breadth casting a shadow.

He reached first for my hands and pulled off my leather riding gloves. Then with an arch of his brow, he knelt on one knee, tapping the side of one boot until I gripped his shoulder and lifted my foot. He took off each boot then swiftly undid my belt and jeans and pushed them roughly down my legs, taking my cotton underwear along with them. He didn't pause to stare, didn't say a word as he waited while I stepped free of my clothing. Then he stood, hands going to the buttons of my plaid shirt, opening them with determined efficiency, and then dragging my sports bra over my head and off my arms.

His gaze raked my nude body, and then he turned and walked back to his bags. He shook soap and shampoo from a plastic carrier and walked to the river's edge where he dropped them on the rocks before striding into the water.

I worried that he hadn't been impressed by what he saw. I wasn't overly endowed. My breasts suited my lean frame. I was well muscled, my ass nicely rounded, but not excessively so. And my legs were long. My best feature, or so I'd been told by the men I'd slept with.

He hadn't given me the benefit of a single compliment. Still, my nipples tightened; the tips stung with anticipation. A heavy pulse throbbed between my legs while moisture slid down my channel.

I glared his way and strode for the water. The bottom of the creek bed was rocky, and I winced when I stepped on a sharp stone. But the coolness of the water was refreshing compared to the heat of the air. I kept my groan of appreciation as quiet as I could and turned away from Zane, giving him my back as I ducked beneath the surface to wet my hair. When I came up, I swiped at my eyes to clear them then gasped when hands slid around my waist and lifted me, dragging me against a hard chest and belly. A thick cock snuggled between my buttocks.

I stood rigid, confused, and began to get irritated. "I don't like you very much," I whispered.

He didn't respond, unless one considered the upward scrape of large hands as they enclosed my breasts an answer. His unwillingness to talk had me frowning. I glanced over my shoulder. "Don't you care that I'm mad at you?"

His mouth curved. Just a slight smile. Not quite a smirk. And it fascinated me.

His fingers clamped harder around my breasts, kneading them, his thumbs and forefingers pinching the tips, lightly at first, then harder, stinging me and causing me to lean harder against his chest as I drew in a hissing breath.

I barely noticed the knee sliding between my thighs, not until I sagged, straddling it. With hard muscle pressed against my engorged cunt lips, I hissed again—and dipped—rubbing against him.

His hands smoothed down my belly. One folded over my mound, the other scooped into the corner where thigh and swollen labia met. Thumbs parted me and cool water invaded the opening of my channel a second before fingers pushed inside.

I tried to remain quiet and still, but the inward stroke of his long fingers drew a groan, and I arched my back, my bottom pushing hard against his cock. I reached over my shoulder to grip his long hair and pull.

He finger-fucked me with slow glides until my hips undulated, following his motions. His mouth lowered to my ear. "I want you on hands and knees on the bank." His hands glided away. His thigh retreated.

A nudge against my backside sent me forward, stumbling toward the riverbank, and I fell forward, crawling to the edge, my breasts dipping into the water, my ass raised high. I spread my knees and waited, not glancing behind me because any sign of masculine satisfaction, a widening smirk for instance, would have tilted me toward anger. I was hungry. Needy. And if he wasn't going to take me, I would find my own damn satisfaction.

Leaning on one hand, I cupped my pussy and slid my middle finger inside, gasping at the pleasure, knowing he watched.

Water sloshed behind me. Hands roughly gripped my ass. I reached deeper between my legs and wrapped my fingers around his thick shaft to pull him toward me.

A gust of laughter sounded, but I wasn't going to let his humor over my impatience slow me down. I pushed back and pulled him closer, fit his crown at my opening and circled to take him inside.

I withdrew my hand and lowered my chest, giving him permission to thrust, waiting while I held my breath.

He pressed forward, but not deeply, sinking only an inch more inside.

My pussy clenched around him, and I dropped my head to the wet sand. I panted so hard my breaths were nearly ragged sobs. A hand smoothed over my ass, dipped into the hollow above it, then glided up to my shoulder. Fingers dug into my scalp, twisting, and then jerking on my hair.

I cried out, coming up on my arms and curving my neck to ease the sting.

Only then did he slam deep. The tension of his fingers never relented, the painful tug kept my back arched, my ass raised high, and he powered into me, slamming deep and hard, his balls banging against the tops of my folds. My neglected clit swelled, and I wriggled, sobbing openly now, because the strength and depths of his thrusts were a harsh tease. He didn't intend for me to orgasm. He withheld the rasp of a fingertip and my posture prevented me from relieving the painful ache myself.

Still my pussy softened, grew lushly hot. My buttocks warmed to the slap of his flesh against mine. My nipples tightened while my breasts grew hard. I'd come like a rocket if he'd show me the slightest mercy.

His hand released my hair. His cock pulled free.

My chest sank to the sand, and I dragged in deep breaths, waiting until they grew steadier before I scrambled forward and turned to give him my meanest glare.

His expression was set. His gaze shuttered. If not for his thick, reddened erection and the tightness of his jaw, I might have believed him unmoved.

A deep inhalation expanded his chest. And I knew. The next move was mine. I lay back half in and out of the water and spread my legs, lifting my knees and using my fingers to spread my folds.

I let him look, waited as his breaths deepened and his nostrils flared. My pussy clenched—something his watchful eyes couldn't miss. And then I reached back my free hand and slipped it under my head. Letting him know, I was his, that I surrendered everything—pride and pleasure—for the privilege of giving him the use of my body.

His Adam's apple bobbed around a hard swallow. His glance trailed from my breasts to my open legs, then back up, locking with my steady gaze. I slowly tugged up my folds, exposing my clit to the air, letting it grow rounder, harder, and I stretched the muscles of my inner thighs to present my clit, my pussy—a supplicant.

Who was this woman? I liked to ride a man. Take my pleasure. But here I was, offering myself. Hoping he'd show me mercy and claim me. "Take me," I pleaded aloud.

Zane's black gaze burned. He crawled between my spread thighs and slipped his palms beneath my ass. When his head lowered and he tongued the edges of my folds, I held my breath.

Without looking up, he pushed away my fingers and replaced them with his own, lifting my folds to bare the ripe knot. The first tap of his tongue had me closing my thighs, trying to trap the sensation, trying to hold him right there.

Fingers stroked inside me. Two thick digits, rooting deeply, swirling. Lush, wet sounds, not unlike the lapping of the water at my bottom, rose. His fingers withdrew only to be followed by three twisting deeper.

My opening burned, stretching to accommodate him. The relentless push and pull juiced me up, eased me open. And then he was adding another, his fingers cupped to push inside.

"No, no, no," I chanted, unsure if I could take more. But my hips pumped, inviting the penetration.

He grunted, ignoring me, and then pushed deeper while he continued to tongue my clit.

Fuck, his whole hand was inside me. My head thrashed. I smoothed my free hand over my lower belly, stroking the top of my mound and then his face, urging him on until he pushed deeper.

I keened, holding my pelvis still as he slowly pushed a couple of inches deeper then pulled back.

"Too much," I whimpered.

"Am I hurting you?"

"Yeah, so good...so fucking good."

His hand pulled free, and he plunged upward, covering me. His weight blanketed me, pushing me into the dirt, but I didn't care. Everywhere he touched me I burned, no place hotter than my cunt where his cockhead teased just my opening.

He rolled his knuckles over my lips and I licked them, tasting me, while I kept my gaze locked with his.

His eyes closed, his expression tightening. When he opened them again, there was no mistaking the need burning there, mirrors of my own. "I wasn't sure you'd be into this."

"Into what?" I asked, breathlessly waiting for him to move.

"Letting me play with you."

"Now I feel like a mouse."

"Am I the cat, batting you between my paws?"

I licked his knuckle again trailing my tongue over the strong ridges. "You've just spoken more words to me than you have all the time we've been out here."

His eyes narrowed as he studied my face.

But I was stubborn too. I jutted my chin and waited.

His lips curled up at one corner. "My brother said I should stay away from you. That he could see wildness in me whenever I looked at you."

"When have you looked at me?"

"That night the couple got separated when the river swept through their camp."

"You never looked at me."

"You came out of the water after swimming the rope to the sandbar to help the wife cross. I could see your nipples. Every man could. My brother said I looked ready to pounce."

I opened my mouth wider to drag in air. "I wish you had. Why didn't you want me coming with you to look for the boys?"

"I had to make some noise. Make sure you were mad at me. Only way I could keep from pulling you off your horse to fuck you standing."

My heartbeat thudded hard against my chest walls. "I wasn't ever mad. Fact is, when I get irritated with you, I just get hornier." I raised my eyelids and let a grin stretch my mouth.

He smiled slowly, his harsh, rugged features softening. "I'm going to fuck you now."

"'Bout time. Thought you'd forgotten where your cock is."

"I'm gonna set up camp here. Might stay a couple days."

I frowned. "I have to get back to work."

He shook his head. "When you didn't arrive with the helo and the boys, my brother called your boss. Told him you wanted to take some time off."

"You were pretty sure of yourself."

"About some things."

"It's important that we do things your way?"

"Yeah. I like bein' in charge."

I swallowed hard, surprised at how much I liked hearing that. "I'm not sure...what you mean."

"Yeah, you do." He brushed a hair from my face and tucked it behind my ear. "You want me to own you, Melanie. You want me to tell you when to strip, when to suck me, when to bend over and take it. And you know I'll give it to you good."

I shook my head, shock rattling through me. "I'm not like that. Never have been. A little wrestling's fine, but I'm not... some submissive."

His smile was undiminished. "I can't wait to tie you down and lick every inch of your skin. Would you like a blindfold when I do it?"

My eyes widened, and I dug my fingertips into his shoulder. But I wasn't pushing him away or withholding my words. My mouth was dry, my tongue stuck to the roof.

He leaned down and pressed a surprisingly soft kiss against my mouth. "We have time to explore. You'll be spendin' more of yours at my ranch."

"Will I?" I asked, surprised my voice rasped like a rusty hinge.

"Your days off. Your nights. I'm gonna prove everything I've said."

My pussy squeezed around his thickness.

"Are you eager to begin?"

I shifted my legs from underneath his, opening to him.

He shook his head. "Be right back."

He rolled off, coming gracefully to his feet, and walked to his saddle. He gripped the horn and swung it up, returning to me. He tossed it to the ground. "Bend over it."

I came up on my elbows, locked gazes with him and tilted my chin. "Make me."

Before I had time to add a smile to the dare, he was on me, hands flipping me to my belly then grasping my wrists behind my back as he pushed me over the saddle. My lower belly rode the curve. My chest was shoved against the dirt, my nipples bitten by rocks. My hands were raised high behind me, leaving me no room for maneuvering. With his free hand, he shoved apart my thighs. And then his cock slid between my cheeks and I worried for a second he'd decide on a different sort of punishment, but his cock slid into my folds, found my center and shoved inside.

He rocked against me, still holding up my arms while he braced himself on one hand stuck in the dirt beside my shoulder.

I could see him from the corner of my eye, liked the feral hardness of his jaw, the way his lips pulled away from his teeth.

While he was rough with me, he wasn't abusive, seeming to know just how much tension my shoulders could take, how hard to thrust.

My cunt was juiced, burning from the friction. My breasts were being scraped raw by the sand as his sharp thrusts pushed me forward and back.

The restrained violence wasn't enough. "More, please, Zane."

He released my wrists to slide a hand beneath me. To please him, I clasped my freed hands behind me, and continued to lie against the dirt waiting for the pleasure I knew he'd give me.

A finger flicked my clit, and I jerked, widening my thighs, trying to get my knees beneath me. With his weight and thrusts keeping me pinned, his fingers plucked at my nub, squeezing and scraping.

My clit was sensitive, so engorged, every rough touch electric. I groaned and grunted, rubbing my chest in the sand, wriggling my butt because that was all the movement he'd allow.

"Now, sweetheart," he whispered, "come now."

He toggled my clit and I exploded, crying out, shuddering and jerking, chanting his name. When I finally fell still, he kissed my shoulder and pulled away. Gentle hands rolled me. He thrust his arms beneath my back and knees and rose with me in his arms, carrying me into the water.

Once there, he let my feet drop and gripped me under my arms.

I didn't need instruction. His cock was insistent, poking at my belly. I wrapped my legs around his waist and eased down on him, resting my cheek on his shoulder while he filled me again.

Grit floated away from my chest as I rubbed my breasts against him. "I'm going to have a rash."

"Sorry. I have ointment I'll rub into them."

"I don't mind. My nipples are on fire," I murmured, smoothing my cheek on his hot skin.

"Can barely think, much less talk. Have a one-track mind when it comes to you." He loosened his arms around me, enough that I could lean away and look into his face. "Ride me."

I stared, finally deciphering that hard, impassive expression of his. He held himself still because he waited for me to make up my mind that he was what I wanted—because once I committed, he wasn't going to turn me loose.

I gripped his shoulders and lifted myself, bringing my face close. "A girl likes to know she rates a kiss, Zane."

His eyes closed. "Sorry."

"Had your mind on more important things," I drawled. "I get that."

His lids lifted a fraction, and he returned my stare. "Belonging to me won't mean I won't listen." He bent his head, and his lips met mine. The kiss was chaste, a gentle rub. He pulled away.

I cupped his ears and pulled on them. "That wasn't nearly what I needed." Slanting my head, I gave him a real kiss, sucking on his lips until he gasped, then thrusting my tongue inside to sweep along his tongue. I liked his taste. Liked the way he pulled on my tongue and then bit my lips. When he broke the kiss, I slowly blinked open my eyes to find him watching me again.

Hands squeezed my buttocks and pulled me down his cock. I grinned because he was forcing me again. And then I moaned because I adored the way he filled me—impatient to thrust deep. I didn't mind he was in a hurry to feel my walls squeeze around him. I was every bit as greedy. With the water churning around us and sunlight dipping beyond the edge of the canyon, I surrendered.

SKIN DEEP

Randi Alexander

Layne Starwood stepped into the aptly named Wrong Turn
Bar. If she hadn't been given detailed directions, she never
would have found it. And if it hadn't been for her ex-fiancé,
Mitchell, the jackass, she'd be here with her girlfriends enjoying
her Cowboy Country Bachelorette Party.

Outside, thunder cracked and rain poured from the sky. She
hoped the storm would pass before nightfall. She'd just walked a
quarter mile from the motel on the hottest, muggiest afternoon
Colorado had ever experienced, just so she could get sloppy
drunk and wouldn't have to drive back.

Her eyes adjusted to the dim interior. To her right, the stage
and dance floor took up half the building. Empty booths lined
the other three walls. The Wrong Turn boasted a big, square
bar of heavy wood but only three stools were occupied. On the
left side corner, facing her, a cowboy sat with his head tipped
down over a beer. Kitty-corner on the other end, an older couple
squinted, probably trying to see who she was.

The bartender looked up from the cash register, his military haircut graying at the temples. "Welcome."

She stepped forward. "Thanks." A row of five empty bar stools stood with their backs to her. She pulled out the middle one and looked to her left. Bad choice. She was directly in the cowboy's line of sight, and he was definitely staring. She got that a lot: curvy with long, red hair and green eyes, guys made a point of ogling.

Too late to move somewhere else, though. She didn't want to offend the man. She sat and slung her purse strap over the back of the chair while sending a shallow smile to the cowboy.

He touched a finger on the brim of his black hat.

As her vision acclimated to the light, she barely caught herself from blanching.

Part of his face was mottled, as though from burns. A puckered scar ran from the side of his nose down through his lip, as though his skin had been ripped in half then sewn back together. The hand wrapped around his beer was missing half an index finger.

Layne looked away quickly. The poor guy probably got stared at far too often. She smothered a wry chuckle. The two of them were the perfect pair for people to eyeball.

The bartender tossed a cardboard coaster down in front of her, cleverly getting it to spin a few times. "What'll it be, ma'am?"

If she'd been here with her girlfriends, they'd be ordering cosmos and margaritas until the bartender wished they'd go somewhere else. But, that'd been the draw of the place. For six country music-loving girls from inner city Denver, finding this bar only a few hours' drive away, and the cute little motel within walking distance, had sounded like the perfect party.

The bartender cleared his throat.

"Sorry. Um…" After her walk, something cold sounded good.

She gestured toward the cowboy. "I'll have what he's having."

Cowboy looked up and a corner of his damaged mouth curved. His lips were full and manly despite the scar. He downed the last inch of his beer.

"Actually…" Impetuous was always fun. "Let me buy a round for the whole bar."

"The *whole* bar?" The bartender laughed. "You got it." He walked away and stuck a glass under the tap.

"Thank you, miss." The cowboy's voice was heavy and quiet.

"You're welcome." She turned then smiled at him. She was going to be here a few hours, and the cowboy looked about as lonely as she felt. May as well make a friend. "I'm not accustomed to your fine country manners, so please call me Layne."

"Layne." He dipped his head. "I'm Kyle."

The bartender brought them glasses of beer and walked away with Kyle's empty.

She took a sip and let the cool bubbles float over her tongue and down her throat. She liked beer. Mitchell, the jackass, had asked her not to drink it at his company functions or when they were out with friends. He'd said wine and cocktails were much more upscale. "Go to hell," she murmured. Picking up her glass, she drained half of it.

"Pardon?" Cowboy tipped his hat back on his head, shedding light on his face. His eyes were a startling robin's egg blue.

Lovely actually.

She shook her head. "Just toasting my ex." Oh hell, why had she brought that up?

The bartender knocked twice on the bar in front of her. "Elsie and Garth thank you for the beer."

How cute. Elsie and Garth. "They're very welcome." She sighed, relaxing into the cozy feel of the homey place.

The bartender walked the few steps to the back and pressed buttons on the cash register.

Layne glanced at Kyle. "So, y'all from around here?" She'd tried for a country accent, but had gone way too far south. Like all the way to Texas.

"I am." The cowboy nodded once. "I have a few cows on a couple acres west of here."

"Ha!" Turning, the bartender grinned at Kyle.

Kyle ignored him. "You?"

"From Denver." Where her girlfriends and family were all spending too much time worrying about her since Marshall, the jackass, broke their engagement two weeks ago. Three weeks before the wedding.

She'd spent a week canceling arrangements and a week feeling sorry for herself. This morning, she'd packed her bag and gotten the hell out of town. She'd never canceled her motel reservation for some reason. She looked toward the cowboy. "I'm running away from home."

He lifted his dark brows. "Good for you."

She laughed, the first real laugh she'd had in months—since things had started going bad between her and the jackass. "I'm about as far from Denver as I could get without running into another big city."

"Yep." He tugged his hat back down over his forehead. "Not many folks can even find this place."

The bartender walked away, whistling a country song about friends in low places.

She looked toward the stage. "I came to hear the band." It was theoretically true. Her girlfriend was a fan of Lone Trail. Layne had never gotten the chance to hear them because the jackass didn't like country music, and had found ways to monopolize her time to the point that she rarely saw her friends anymore.

The cowboy looked at the wall clock. "You've got about a four-hour wait."

That was her plan. Get lumpy drunk, hear the band, meander back to her room before dark, and sleep it off.

Her phone rang. She pulled it out of her purse. Her mother. "Hi."

"Are you almost there? There are storms rolling out of the Rockies."

"Yes, I'm close. A couple hours away, but the roads are clear here. Must have missed the rain." As she glanced out the small window at the deluge, she caught Kyle's stare, and he looked away. "I'll text you when I get there."

"Kiss that new baby for me."

"I will. Bye, Mom." She ended the call and sighed. "You're probably wondering why—"

"Nope." Kyle held up a hand. "None of my business." He shifted in his seat.

Maybe it was the beer, or maybe it was his quiet strength, but she wanted to talk to him. "I needed to get away. Everyone's been smothering me since...since we broke off the engagement." He'd broken it off, but she probably should have done it a year ago.

"So you *are* running away from home. Literally." He smiled, showing straight white teeth.

"I literally am." Since she was getting to ready to settle in for a good, long pity party, she probably needed to take care of business first. "'Scuse me." Grabbing her purse, she wandered to the ladies' room. There she washed her hands, staring at her reflection in the mirror. She'd taken three weeks off her job at the brewery; one for the pre-wedding week and two for the honeymoon. What was she going to do with herself for twenty-one days?

When she got back to the bar, another beer sat next to her quarter-full one. "Where did this come from?"

He shrugged one shoulder and tipped his head down. "No idea."

"Thank you, Kyle." She sat one bar stool closer to him and shifted her beers in front of her. "Are you here for the band, too?"

Giving her a sidelong glance, he lifted a brow. "Four hours early? No." He took a drink of brew. "I was in town doing some banking. Thought I'd stop for one on the way home."

She downed the rest of her first beer and sat the glass on the bar rail. "That must be your big-ass truck out there." She leaned to her right to look at the elderly couple. "Elsie and Garth don't look like they need a fifth-wheel hitch with dualies."

"You know your trucks." Kyle tapped the blunt end of his half finger against his beer glass.

"I do. Always wanted one, but..." The jackass wasn't interested in camping or horses or anything to do with the outdoors. She'd given up too many of her pleasures and dreams for him.

"Well..." The cowboy set down his empty glass and stood.

Her stomach dropped. She didn't want him to leave. "I suppose you have a wife and kids waiting for you."

Beneath his tan, the cowboy's face went white.

The bartender walked toward them. "Leavin', Kyle?"

"No." His lips flattened. "Pour me one more, would ya, Ben?" He walked off toward the bathrooms.

Ben stared after him until the bathroom door squeaked shut. "Huh."

She leaned closer. "I think I said something wrong. I asked about his wife and kids."

With a sorrowful look, Ben let out his breath. "He's a widower. No kids, either."

Her heart thudded. What a stupid thing for her to say. "I'm so sorry."

Ben shrugged. "You couldn't have known. It was a couple years ago."

"He looks so young." Close to her age, she'd bet.

"Right around thirty." He gestured to Kyle's beer glass. "Ever since, he comes in for a beer once a week and we talk. Must be a special occasion today." The bartender winked at her. "I've never seen him have more than two."

The bathroom door squeaked.

Ben walked away and grabbed a clean glass.

Kyle slid onto his bar stool and laced his fingers together in front of him on the bar. "Suppose he told you, huh?"

"He did." She swallowed the ache that snuck up her throat. "I'm really sorry. It was insensitive of me to—"

"No. Actually, it was a compliment." He locked his blue gaze with hers. "Most women think I'm too ugly to be married."

Her mouth dropped open.

Ben set down the fresh beer, glanced at Layne with a grimace, then left with Kyle's empty.

She didn't know whether to cry or slap him. "If you're trying to make me feel bad, you're doing a good job." Her voice quavered just a little. Hell, she thought she was hosting the only pity party today, but there was Kyle, throwing one of his own.

He scrubbed a palm down his face.

"I'll take my beer and go sit with Elsie and Garth." She grabbed her purse off the back of her stool. "Leave you to your own company."

"No, please." He reached toward her and set his hand, palm-down, on the bar. "I apologize. That was uncalled for."

She wanted to take his hand, wanted to touch him...but that was just crazy. How could her heart go out to someone that

quickly? "All right, cowboy." She hung her purse on the back
of the stool to her left, the one closest to his, and slid onto it,
hauling her beer and coaster with her. "We've got..." She looked
at the clock. "Three hours and forty-five minutes to have a nice,
quiet talk. Since we're both evidently in need of someone to
unload onto, and we're already in *this deep*, I think we should
just go for it."

He lifted a brow. "You do, huh?"

"I do." She settled in. "And I'll start." She told him about
her ex-fiancé and her broken wedding plans. She admitted she'd
snuck out of Denver that morning and told everyone she was
going to visit a friend who'd just had a baby.

He told the sad story of his wife of three years becoming ill
and dying within months. When he talked about the last couple
of years of his life, she had to wipe away a few tears. She could
tell he was lonely. He never mentioned how he came by the
scars.

They sipped beer and talked about the plans and dreams
that had fallen apart, and the futures that looked too daunting
to give any solace.

Layne's strategy to get shit-faced drunk didn't interest her
anymore as they nursed their beers and later snacked on a couple
of Ben's burger baskets.

Fifteen minutes before the band was supposed to start, the
musicians came in and set up their instruments. She glanced
around. More than half the booths were filled, waitresses carried
drinks and food, and Ben had a woman helping him behind the
bar. When had all this happened? She glanced at Kyle.

He blinked as he looked around. Evidently, they'd been deep
in their own little world, and had filtered out everything else.
"Be right back." He headed to the men's room.

She watched him this time: his slim hips, long legs and V-shaped torso were everything she'd expected in a real cowboy.

"Can I buy you a beer?" A young man, dressed for a Saturday night at a honky-tonk, squeezed in between her bar stool and the empty one next to her.

"No, thank you. I'm leaving in a few minutes." She turned away.

"My buddies and I were hoping you'd stay." He gestured to a pack of five guys all staring at her like she was fresh meat. "Dance with us."

"No. Thank you." She used her firm voice, the one that always sent guys fleeing.

"Okay, but when you get tired of that old butt face cowboy, we'll be waitin' for you."

"What?" Her blood pressure spiked. "You know..." She turned to face him. "It's bullshit like that that makes me hate pretty boys like you." And he was pretty. "That cowboy is the nicest man I've met in a hell of a long time, and for you to judge him on his skin instead of his soul is narrow-minded and ignorant."

Pretty Boy looked up, over her head, and with a sinking sensation in her gut, she knew Kyle was back.

The kid's cheeks flamed red and he walked away.

She turned to the cowboy.

He stood next to his bar stool. "You don't need to fight my battles."

He spoke softly, but she knew he was angry, his bright blue eyes had darkened. Damn, she'd insulted him again. How could she tell him she was fighting her own battles, too? She'd always been the pretty one, the one men asked to dance first, never her girlfriends. Marshall, the jackass, had always commented on how lovely she was, never how smart or funny or interesting.

She'd had enough of acting like an idiot. As Ben walked by,

she gestured to him. "Can you call me a taxi?" She didn't want to walk in the rain, and who knew what that pack of pretty boys was capable of.

"Okay. You're a taxi." He grinned but shook his head. "We've got nothing like that out here, but..."

"I'll drive you." Kyle's voice sounded too quiet.

Ben nodded. "I can vouch for him. You'll be safe with him."

She risked a glance at the cowboy.

He seemed to have drawn back into his quiet zone. Pulling out his wallet, he settled up for all their drinks.

She didn't dare insult his manhood again by offering to pay her share, so she worked at finishing her last beer.

"All right, cowboys and cowgirls!" The band member's voice came through the sound system. "We're Lone Trail, and we're glad to be here tonight." A smattering of applause and the sound of guitars tuning filled the room. "We've got some special occasions tonight." He held up a piece of paper. "It's Flo Bauman's fiftieth birthday today. Where's Flo?"

Shouts from the far end of the bar revealed where her party was going strong.

"Okay, and we've got Layne's bachelorette party. Where's Layne and the girls?"

Silence.

Layne looked at Kyle. His eyes were wide and staring right at her. She grimaced. "So...now might be a good time to leave, don't you think?"

His lips twitched in a partial smile as he came around the corner of the bar, holding out his hand.

She placed hers in his and the zing of awareness rattled her. She stood and found herself almost a foot shorter than the cowboy.

He placed his hand on her lower back and guided her toward

the door. His height and the sure way he led her caused her heartbeat to rev. As they passed the pretty boys, she could almost smell the testosterone wafting off Kyle, as if he was marking what was his.

The thought of being *his* made her core jitter with delight. His hand on her back warmed her through her whole body. The rain had slowed, and as he helped her up into his truck, his hands lingered on her just long enough to make her crazy for more of the cowboy.

He slid into the driver's seat and turned the ignition. "Your bachelorette party, huh?"

"I must have forgotten to tell you that part." She'd intentionally left it out of her story. "Guess it makes me look kind of…" She stared out the side window. "Pathetic." Driving all this way for a canceled party. Pathetically crazy.

"Hey." His voice came out stern.

She turned to look at him.

"I'd say you were brave to do this. Seeking closure, right?" He got the truck moving toward the motel and looked at her out of the corner of his eye. "I'm impressed. You've got a lot more going for you than your looks."

She sucked in a breath. He was pretty damn amazing. Every instinct told her she could trust him, and every intuition said she shouldn't let him slip away.

Kyle pulled up in front of room seven, jumped out, and helped her down from the high seat. He walked her to her door, opened it and flipped the switch to turn on the lamp. He leaned in and glanced around her room to make sure it was safe.

"Can I pay you for the ride?" They stood outside under the overhang as rain formed a wall, sealing them alone together.

He looked down at her, his gorgeous eyes narrowing with a

sexy look. He took her wrist and tugged her close. "Yeah, you can."

Oh hell, yes! She wanted this cowboy, every perfectly macho inch of him. Wrapping her hand around the nape of his neck, she pressed her breasts to his chest and went up on tiptoes.

He groaned and lowered his lips to hers.

Her skin flushed hot, her heart thudded, and between her legs, her pussy tingled and ached.

His kiss took everything she had, his tongue feasting on her, tasting and teasing.

The earth moved, but wait—it was him walking her backward into her room. The door slammed and he pressed her back against it.

His steaming-hot body flattened against her front as the door cooled her back. His kiss slowed while he sucked her tongue into his mouth, encouraging her to explore and sample him. Beer and spices from the burger, and a male taste all his own combined on her tongue. She ran her tongue over his lip, loving the texture of his scar.

He ground the rise in his jeans into her mound, hot and hungry.

She needed to be closer. Grabbing the front of his shirt, she pulled and buttons popped.

He tossed his hat, ripped away the rest of his shirt, then went for her T-shirt, ripping it down the front.

Animal instinct arose in her and her hips bucked forward, demanding his intrusion into her, his hard cock into her wet slit. He ripped the front of her bra in two, mumbling, "I'll pay for it." Her breasts spilled out and her puckered nipples prickled in the cool air, then warmed as his gaze locked on them.

"I don't give a damn about my clothes." She reached for his belt.

Taking her nipple into his mouth, the heat, combined with incredibly talented sucking, blasted shivers to her core, tingling through her channel, slicking her pussy.

When he moved to her other nipple, she cried his name. Oh god, she didn't even know his last name. She didn't even know if she cared. She finally got his belt unbuckled, his zipper down, and she slid her hand into his underwear, into the heat surrounding his cock. Hard and thick, his staff pulsed against her palm. Her mouth watered and her cunt convulsed.

He tore open a condom packet with his teeth. "Jesus, Layne, I've got to have you now." His eyes burned dark and feral. "I need to be inside you, but I promise I've got slow lovin' for you, too." His breath panted from his chest. "It just can't be slow right now."

His words, his intense stare sent shimmies of desire racing through her. "Take me, cowboy, hard and fast."

Her words sent him wild. He had her jeans and underwear off her in seconds, got himself naked and the condom on even quicker, and his hands grabbed her ass and lifted her higher.

Oh fuck, he was going to do her right here, right against the motel door. Her body quivered with delight. She lifted her legs as he jerked his hips and the thick head of his cock pressed against her pussy.

He shook his head. "Layne, what is it about you that makes me crazy for you?"

"What?" Her mind wouldn't process as she clung to his shoulders and moved her hips forward to take him inside her slit.

He thrust upward, into her, filling her.

"Ahh." The slick, sweet stretching ache of his big cock taking her, shoving ball-deep inside her, ran blazing shivers up her spine.

Using his hands to guide her hips, he drove into her, a rolling motion that ground him against her, tweaking her clit with each pump. He kissed her neck, sucking and nibbling. Her nipples grated against his curly chest hair. Every touch of his body on hers sizzled like a live wire, sending her closer to climax.

This cowboy was all man, rough, rugged, taking what he wanted, but giving her more ecstasy than she'd ever known.

"Aw lady, you feel so fucking good." He sucked her earlobe and bit, turning the darkness behind her eyelids into white flashes.

Her hands ran over his shoulders and back. Big muscles flexed as he took his pleasure, filling her with mind-numbing heat. She thrust her fingers into his brown hair and pulled his head back to look at him in the dim lamplight. "You are too goddamn sexy." She meant it, she felt it, soul deep. "Now make me come, cowboy, make me scream."

His lips curled back from gritted teeth and his hips double-timed, pistoning his cock into her slick pussy, hitting her deep. "Whatever you want, Layne. Anything I've got."

The motion turned her nipples into firecrackers that sparked through her bloodstream. The drilling of his cock shot ripples of delight up her back. With a bone-rattling shake, she broke free, dove backward over a cliff, and cried out his name. Tumbling through sensations, her skin burned and her core contracted achingly tight around his pumping cock.

He shouted and grunted as his body tensed and the thrusts of his staff in her pussy became erratic and wild.

She clung to him as her mind spun in freefall through currents of ecstasy that took her breath from her.

As his movements slowed, she drifted back toward aware-ness, her head resting on his shoulder. His lips pressed kisses along her neck and his heart thudded hard and fast against her chest.

She breathed deep, smelling sex and sweat and the fresh-air scent of his skin. "That was a religious experience, cowboy."

He chuckled. "Lady, you made me believe again." His words came out quiet but packed a charge. She knew he had to be referring to her comment, but could he also be talking about a relationship? About...love?

The word ricocheted around inside her brain. She could easily see herself giving him a chance.

He stepped back, holding her tightly, and walked to the bed. Setting her carefully on the comforter, he leaned over her and kissed her quickly. "Be right back." He walked into the bathroom.

She watched him, searching for the words to ask him if they could do this again someday. Maybe meet back here, or in Denver, or halfway between. She wasn't ready to say good bye, but what was he thinking?

He came out of the bathroom and lay next to her, turning her on her side to spoon behind her.

She snuggled in, but then her heart lurched. Was this a way for him to hide his scars?

"What you said back at the bar." His voice rumbled from his chest. "To that kid. That meant a lot to me. I've looked like this since I was a kid. Women don't..."

Closing her eyes, she let tenderness wash through her, let her words flow without worrying she'd scare him off. "I spoke the truth. You are the most interesting, kindest man I've ever met."

"You don't strike me as someone who'd just say that to be nice."

She turned to lie on her back and looked at him. "I'm not, Kyle. It's true."

His gaze met hers, his brow furrowing. "I want to get to

know you. Damn it, I'm not willing to let you go tonight."

Her breath hitched as her chest flooded with warmth. "What are you proposing, cowboy?"

"Come to the ranch with me. Right now. I want you in my bed." His thumb traced her lip. "I want to make love to you as the sun comes up. We can watch it as it hits the mountains. It's as beautiful as anything you've ever seen."

How could she resist? "I'd love to. I just have to put on some *unripped* clothes and grab my suitcase." She gave him a blazing smile. "I'll follow you."

"No. You'll ride with me. I'll send a couple ranch hands back to get your car."

Now *her* brows furrowed. "Ranch hands? On a three-acre ranch with two cows?"

His smile was crooked, almost shy. "I guess it's a little bigger than that."

"By how much?" Was this cowboy a major-league rancher?

"Well, deeded acres, about twenty thousand." He blinked a couple times. "With the leased land, over three-hundred thousand."

"What?" She couldn't imagine that much space, that many beautiful spots to ride... "Wait, do you have horses?"

"I do. You ride?"

"I do." She gave him a loud kiss on the lips. "Cowboy, you may want to rethink your offer. You may never, ever get rid of me if you take me to your ranch."

His face grew serious. "Promise?"

She nodded as her heart skipped a beat. "This runaway may just be done traveling."

DROP TWO TEARS IN A BUCKET

Shoshanna Evers

E llie had expected more. Instead, she sat at her kitchen table, alone in her home, and didn't cry. She had no tears left to be shed over her ex-husband, not even today, when the divorce was made officially final. He'd left their home and their marriage long before a document told her it was over.

The late afternoon sunlight reflected off the snow-topped mountains around her cabin and filled her kitchen with low light. Her ex hadn't wanted to keep their Montana cattle ranch, and she supposed she could get a good price for the acreage and the herd. But the isolation suited her. No neighbors. No city lights.

Just the men who drove along the unpaved road every morning before dawn to work. They were tight friends and hard workers. They handled everything except the books, which had been her husband's job until he left.

"Ellie?"

At the sound of her foreman, knocking and opening the

door at the same time, she looked at the clock. "Little early for quittin' time, Shayne," she said, but without any real concern. The guys never left unless their work was done.

"Janet's water broke," he said, talking about another cowboy's wife.

Ellie tried to smile, but to her horror, a sob escaped her lips.

"Hey now!" Shayne rushed to her side, his muscular young body pressing against her. "She'll be fine, Ell. It ain't like she's never done this before."

"Of course," Ellie said, looking away. "And of course, if Dean's gotta go, then he should go."

"He's already gone." Shayne took her face in one hand and turned her head toward him, something he'd never done before.

Ellie felt a frisson of desire but brushed it off immediately. Shayne was a good decade younger than her, and though he didn't have a wife or family yet, she knew it was only a matter of time before some young cowgirl caught him.

Why had a handsome guy like him stayed single for so long?

"Don't think I ever saw you cry before," he said softly.

"I cried when that calf had to be put down."

"Damn, I nearly cried over that one too." He took his hat off and hung it on the back of a chair. "Mind if I sit down?"

Ellie didn't bother answering, since he'd already turned the chair around backward and straddled it, his strong legs seeming to fill her space.

He nodded toward the papers on the table. "I saw the FedEx guy show up earlier. That what I think it is?"

Ellie wiped her eyes with the back of her hand, but her tears were already gone. No more tears for that man. "Yeah. It's official."

"I think that calls for a celebration."

She laughed and shrugged. Shayne had always been good at cheering her up. He even danced with her, back when they all went out to town, while her husband sat at the bar and got drunk. When her favorite cowboy whirled her around, he made her feel young and attractive again.

Then she'd traverse the windy unpaved road back home with her husband and put him to bed while Shayne closed the bar down, dancing with every woman who came in, no doubt.

But he always saved a dance for her.

"Lemme tell you something, Ellie." He rubbed his jaw with his rough, calloused hand. "Best piece of advice I ever got for dealing with trouble."

Ellie cocked her head to the side, running her fingers through her hair—hair that had once been blonde and was now light brown.

"*You're* gonna tell me about trouble?" She laughed and shook her head. "You *are* trouble, boy."

"Yeah I am." Shayne stood from the chair and pushed it aside. "Here it is, and excuse my language for a moment. You ready for some mountain wisdom?" He paused, as if to make sure she was paying attention. "Drop two tears in a bucket—and motherfuck it."

Really.

Ellie burst into laughter. "Drop two tears in a bucket and motherfuck it," she repeated. "That's some honest wisdom, right there."

Shayne grinned and lifted her by the hands from her chair until she stood.

He was a tall man, that cowboy. His body filled her vision, the muscles in his shoulders straining against his work shirt. He smelled like the horses he and the men rode around the property, but she didn't mind. Liked it, actually.

Shayne smelled like home.

"You wanna celebrate?" he asked softly.

She nodded, not quite sure what she was agreeing to.

His rough-skinned hands were gentle as he carefully pushed her hair behind her ears, out of her face. But instead of stopping there, stopping short of doing anything—the way he always did—he left his hand in her hair, slowly pulling it back behind her shoulders and down, so she had no choice but to look up into his handsome face.

"Shayne," she whispered, but he cut off her words with a kiss.

Sandpaper stubble scratched her chin, but the heat of his mouth and lips on hers made her push up onto her tiptoes to give him better access.

"I've been wantin' to do this for so long now," he murmured against her mouth.

He unbuttoned his shirt, slowly, still kissing her, and she ran her hands against the smooth muscular span of his chest. The thud of his heart pulsed against her palm, and she lowered her lips to kiss him there. His skin tasted of salt, and she was hungry for him. For more.

"Would you like to…" Ellie stopped, suddenly shy.

"Hell, yeah," he said, and lifted her against his torso, his shirt open, and carried her like a newborn calf in his arms up the narrow staircase to her bedroom.

She'd long stopped thinking of it as "their" bedroom. Her and her ex-husband's.

The down quilt on the bed was still pulled back from that morning when she'd risen late, way after daybreak.

Shayne set her on the bed and pulled off his boots and dirty jeans, barely giving her time to even realize what was happening.

Shayne was happening. Now. To her.

The best-looking, strongest young man she knew in the world outside of the television set, and he was staring at her like she was some sort of delicious prey to be devoured.

Not that she'd mind being devoured, not by him. Ellie pulled her shirt off, and unclasped her bra, letting her breasts lie heavy against her chest.

"Good Lord in heaven," Shayne said, and climbed onto the bed. "You've been holding out on me."

He took her nipple in his mouth and suckled it, nibbling on the tender peak until she moaned, kicking off her own boots. They fell to the hardwood floor by her bed with a dull thud.

His mouth on her breasts was beyond heaven, the harsh scratch of his stubbled chin rubbing against her delicate skin only serving to increase the pleasure he brought her with his lips.

"Help me," she whispered, unable to take her jeans off with his weight on her.

With an easy maneuver, he unzipped her fly and tugged off her jeans, taking her panties down with them. Ellie hadn't done any grooming down there in a while, since there hadn't been a need to, and she flushed with embarrassment. "Sorry," she said. "Been a long time."

"I like my women natural," he said, and slid his fingers along her labia, pushing her nether lips apart to reveal her clit, already swollen with need. "This is beautiful, right here." He touched her gently, slowly, making her dizzy with need. "You're beautiful."

The lust in his eyes made her believe it. Tonight, she was beautiful.

"You lay back now," he ordered. "It's celebration time. I ain't stoppin' till I hear you scream my name so loud the neighbors can hear."

"Ain't no neighbors," she said breathlessly, slipping easily into his casual way of speaking. Her fingers gripped the cool sheets beneath her hands, grasping as if the world had tilted on its axis.

"That's what I'm talkin' about."

Shayne licked her clit, sucking it into his mouth, and she gasped. No one had touched her there in ages, it seemed. Ripples of pleasure coursed through her as he continued to lave her, pushing a finger deep inside of her and flicking her clit with his tongue. He pushed her thighs apart, holding her there, captured beneath his hands as he tasted her, licked her, nibbled her sensitive bud.

The man had a way with his hands and mouth. Her climax crested, and he sped up the pace.

"Oh my god, Shayne," she cried out, bucking her hips against his face as she came.

He held on, keeping her from closing her legs so he could extend her orgasm, drawing out every last quiver. "There you go, Ell, there you go," he whispered, rising up to her neck, her lips.

She could taste herself on him, the scent of her sex mingling with the scent of horses and man and mountains.

"Do I need a rubber?" he asked.

She shook her head. Ellie was past her baby-making years. She reached down between their naked bodies, and he pressed his cock against her hand, so thick she couldn't wrap her fingers all the way around it.

After the two-year-long drought in her sex life, she drank in his masculinity like rain. "Please," she whispered.

He slowly entered her wetness, pushing forward until he was completely in, filling her, stretching her.

Shayne kissed her face, raining down light, tender kisses,

and rocked his body against hers, his length sliding in and out.

She wrapped her arms around his shoulders and clung to him, letting him ride her as he saw fit, harder, faster, until they were both panting.

The slam of his cock inside her, over and over, shook her body like the ground in a stampede. She thrust her hips up to meet him stroke for stroke, wanting everything he had to give her. Her vaginal walls spasmed around his cock and she moaned with desire, the orgasm wrenching open something within her that she'd kept shut off ever since her husband had walked out.

It was as if a dam had broken inside, as if everything she'd stored up and bottled and pushed away came free at once.

Free.

Freedom here, in Shayne's arms. It was exactly where she wanted to be.

Tears of catharsis filled her eyes and streamed down her cheeks, falling silently on the cotton pillowcase. Yes, the dam had broken, and it felt damn good.

Shayne stopped moving, pushing his weight off of her. "Ellie...did I hurt you?"

She couldn't answer at first, but she shook her head no and smiled up at him. "You are one man who's never, ever hurt me, Shayne."

He kissed her tears, wiping them away.

"Baby, baby," he whispered. "I never will."

A COWBOY
FOR DELILAH

Sabrina York

What a disaster. Delilah glared at her rental car in helpless
frustration. She hated the feeling. She was hardly a frail,
fragile woman. She prided herself on the fact that she was self-
sufficient and didn't need anyone. Counting on others was, after
all, a recipe for disappointment.

Hard, cold experience had taught her that.

Yet here she was. In the boondocks. In six-inch heels. With
a flat tire.

Oh, she could change a fricking tire. Hell, she could rip
out and refurbish a transmission. But the idiots at the wilderness rental car company hadn't bothered to put a jack in the
trunk. She was resourceful...but not that resourceful. Even if
she could channel her MacGyveresque tendencies, there was
nothing out on this barren plain she could use to lever her car
up high enough to do the job.

So here she stood by the side of the road in the middle of
nowhere, in six-inch heels and without cell phone service—the

epitome of a helpless woman. All she needed was slasher music and she could be the star of a horror flick.

A plume of dust blossomed on the horizon and her mood lifted. Oh, thank god. Someone was coming. No one had passed in the two hours since the blowout.

Hopefully, it wasn't a slasher.

The plume grew. A beat-up pickup topped one rise, and then the next. The truck rolled to a stop in front of her crippled Honda.

Oh. Lovely. Her savior had a gun rack.

Delilah covered her mouth and nose as the cloud of dust caught up with the truck and engulfed her. Angie's birthday party had better be worth all this trouble.

She plastered a smile on her face and turned to greet the Good Samaritan. At least, she hoped he was a Good Samaritan. She was quite alone on this deserted stretch of road and—

Oh god.

He unfolded himself from the cab of his truck, and her breath wedged in her throat. He was enormous. And, judging from his ratty chambray shirt, shit-kicker boots and Stetson, he was a cowboy.

She hated cowboys. Selfish, misogynistic sons of bitches. Her fake smile threatened to become a very real grimace.

He stepped closer through the lingering cloud of dust, and Delilah's heart *ker-chunked*. He was gorgeous. Not only was he tall—which she really liked in a man—he was big. Broad and brawny and muscular. His face was a dream from his heavily lashed brown eyes to the intriguing dent on his chin. She had to remind herself why cowboys and city girls didn't mix, but even that couldn't keep her from ogling his forearms. His sleeves were rolled up, just enough to give her a glimpse of defined veins and a sprinkling of dark hair. She loved veiny forearms.

Damn. Why couldn't he have been something other than a cowboy? Or, if he had to be a cowboy, why couldn't he have been an old one...with Dunlap syndrome—where his belly done lapped over his belt?

"Howdy." His voice was deep and smoky.

Delilah couldn't appreciate the sultry timbre. Of all greetings in the universe, *Howdy* was her least favorite.

"Having some trouble?" He whipped off his Stetson to wipe his brow and thick black curls tumbled out.

Curls. Not fair. Why couldn't he be bald?

Delilah cleared her throat. "Flat tire."

He glanced at her car. A dimple exploded on his cheek.

Fuck.

Dimples were her kryptonite.

"Would you like me to change it for you? You do have a spare?"

Yeah. There it was. Sure he was superhot, gorgeous and sexy as hell. But his patronizing tone squelched any simmering temptation she might have been harboring.

That's how it was with cowboys, wasn't it? They saw all women as helpless, idiot creatures stumbling around in six-inch heels, batting their lashes and flashing their boobs and simpering.

Delilah was not a simperer. She was a fuck-you, take-no-prisoners, hard-core lawyer, who could take care of herself just fine.

But she did have a flat. And no jack. She kinda needed his help.

So she batted her lashes. "Um. I think there's a tire thingy in the...what do you call it? Trunk?" She affected a Southern drawl and thrust out her boobage, just for good measure.

It annoyed her that he bought her act. And it kind of didn't.

The bedazzled look in his eyes was a salve to her ego. After Trevor and all. It was nice to know she could still appeal to a man. Even a redneck cowboy.

He loped over to her car—*yes, loped.* She tried not to stare at his ass but his jeans were tight. It was a challenge to look elsewhere. He bent to search the trunk—again, a mighty fine ass—and stood, tipping back his Stetson. His profile, against the bird's-egg-blue backdrop of the sky, stole her breath.

"There's no jack."

"No what?"

He sighed and headed for his truck, pulling out an impressively fancy jack. "This," he said, "is a jack. You use it to lift the carriage up high enough to change the tire."

It was so sweet the way he made his voice all slow and pedantic. You know, so she could understand. Idiot woman that she was.

"Gosh. You're smart." She probably didn't need to gush quite that much, but hell, she hated condescending men. Especially cowboys. But she might as well have fun with this.

He knelt and fitted the jack and started cranking. His muscles bunched, forearms bulging with each pump.

Delilah sighed, and told herself it was only a pretend sigh, but her gaze was riveted to the sight. "You are such a big, strong man."

He flashed a grin at her.

Yeah. Of course he did. Men loved to be told how big and strong they were. She completely ignored the dimples erupting all over his bristled cheek. Did he never shave? "How can I ever repay you?"

He stilled. The glint in his eye was horrifying. Crap. Had she gone too far with her helpless female shtick? She was all alone. On a deserted highway. With an enormous Neanderthal cowboy.

When he tipped his head to the side, her trepidation vanished. He looked more like a mischievous boy than a mad rapist-slasher. "How about a kiss?"

Delilah blinked. "A...what?"

"A kiss. Just a little one."

Her brain fogged over. And it wasn't horror at the prospect of a strange man demanding a kiss on the side of a deserted road that muddied the waters. It was pure exhilaration at the thought of *his mouth* devouring hers, *those arms* wrapping around her, *that massive chest*, warm and hard as he yanked her close...

Aw hell.

Why was she always attracted to the wrong guys? She wanted a man who liked opera and dreamed of traveling to Italy. Not a guy who listened to Country and Western music, spat chew into a bean can, and whose dream of an exciting evening was a night at the local bar playing pool.

"What do you say, ma'am? One kiss, in exchange for my... services?" When she hesitated, he repeated, "A little one."

Why she nodded, she had no clue.

Well, she knew why she nodded—because she was incapable of speech.

Why she *agreed* was the mystery.

Then again, he was superhot. She ached to know how he tasted...and it wasn't as though they would ever see each other again. Besides, if things got out of hand, she had mace. And she knew how to use it.

At her assent, he sprang into action. It was astounding how quickly he changed that tire. He tossed the flat into the trunk, returned his jack to his truck and wiped his hands.

"All done."

Her heart skittered as he stepped closer.

"Time for payment." His voice was a low thrum.

Excitement coursed through her body. She trembled as he cupped her cheek. His palm was rough, calloused. Heat singed her. "O-one k-kiss," she murmured. "A little one."

"I remember." She tasted his breath as he whispered the words.

And then his lips touched hers. Gently. Sweetly. Rubbing back and forth, nibbling, questing. Her pulse thrummed—she felt it...*everywhere.* He delved deeper, nudging her with his tongue. He tasted delicious. Like peppermint and man.

Without thought, she opened her mouth to him, and he entered her.

She'd never enjoyed French kisses before, but this kiss was different. It was divine. Exquisite. It made her want only one thing...more.

He drew back and she captured his nape with desperate fingers. Held him there.

More. More. God, please more.

He complied with her unspoken demand, changing his angle and deepening the kiss. His brawny arms wrapped around her and held her tight. His fingers idly explored the curve of her waist. Then his hand skated higher, curving around the swell of her breast.

A feral groan hummed between them. She wasn't sure if it was his or hers. Hardly cared. Because, just then, his thumb nudged her taut nipple. Her knees went weak, and she collapsed against him.

He lifted his head and stared at her, the lust in his eyes in full flower. A muscle bunched in his cheek. His body pulsated with sexual tension. A look flickered across his face—a look that made her think he was going to kiss her again. An electrifying thrill sizzled through her veins. She shivered.

But then, he released her. Cold seeped in.

"One kiss." This, he whispered. "Thank you, ma'am." He tipped his hat and turned and walked to his truck with a lopsided gait.

She ached to call him back. Demand he finish what he started, but she knew better.

This was a dangerous man. She had to let him go.

Had to never see him again.

Not ever.

A niggle in the region of her heart annoyed her. She knew what would happen if she opened her mouth and said "Wait," or "Come back," or something equally stupid. The end result would be more than an aching heart. It would be utter disaster.

She'd been down that road before.

He paused before he levered into his truck. "I'll follow you for a ways, to make sure you don't have any more trouble. But I'm only going a couple more miles up the road."

His chivalry annoyed her. God damn it. Why couldn't he be a douche like all the rest of them?

She nodded and fished in her purse for the car keys. It gave her something to do. Something other than stare at him and drool. Something to dull those slicing shards of regret.

Damn. She would remember him for a long, long time. She would remember...and wonder.

Shit.

Landon McCoy glared at the little blue car kicking up dust in front of him as he finished the drive to his brother's ranch. He hadn't asked her name.

He should have asked her name.

At least then he'd have something to call her in his dreams when he was fisting his cock tonight, relieving the aching pressure she'd caused.

Or maybe not tonight. Maybe this afternoon.

He was as hard as a rock.

He should have asked for two kisses. If he'd had two kisses, he probably could have bargained for more. Maybe convinced her to tell him her name. Her number. Something other than the thin knowledge she'd rented a car from Skeeter.

Lord, she was a pretty thing, from her jet-black hair to her perfectly pedicured toes. He usually didn't go for bimbos, but this doll could make him forget his own name. She was tall and curvy in all the right places. Her breasts had been warm, firm, sublime. But as amazing as her body was, her face eclipsed it. She was, in a word, gorgeous. There was an elfin cant to her amber eyes hinting at a playful side. Her skin was flawless and her lips...

His thoughts trailed off as he remembered her lips. Their fullness, the velvety texture, her taste. It had taken everything in him to keep to his promise and stop after that one kiss. But what a magnificent kiss it had been.

And he'd never see her again.

They neared the turn for AC Ranch and a little bubble of acid played in his gut. This was it. Where he'd turn, and she'd keep going straight. Where they would part ways for fucking ever.

But then, to his shock, she didn't go straight. She turned. To the left.

Holy crap.

He turned as well, his heart thrumming in his throat.

Because he would.

He would see her again.

And soon.

He pulled up behind her in Cody's driveway and hopped out of his truck. He was going to smile at her and ask if she was lost, but before he could, she leapt out of the Honda and whirled on him, a flare of fear in her eyes.

"Are you following me?" she spat.

Landon blinked. "Following you?" *Shit.* She thought he was a stalker. "No. This is my brother's ranch. He got delayed. He asked me to come by and feed the horses."

Her eyes narrowed. "Your brother's place?" Lord, she could hiss. "What's his name?"

"Cody. Cody McCoy. He and his wife Ange went to Dallas for the week. For her birthday."

The woman, his spitfire angel, crossed her arms over her chest. "Why didn't she mention that when she invited me to come here? For her *birthday?*"

Ah hell. *That's* who she was. "Because it was a surprise. Angie didn't know." Landon took off his Stetson and raked his fingers through his hair. "You must be Delilah."

Confusion tangled with the fury on the exquisite planes of her face. Her brow wrinkled. "How do you know my name?"

"Angie asked me to make you feel at home. She and Cody'll be back tomorrow." He thrust out a hand. "I'm Landon." She didn't take his hand, so he felt compelled to add, "I'm not a stalker."

Incongruously, she laughed. The sound trickled through him. As pretty as she was when she snarled at him, she was even more captivating when she smiled. "All right, Landon McCoy. I believe you."

He grinned. Winked. "There are photos of me in the house if you want to confirm who I am."

Her smile faded. "I said I believe you."

An awkward silence rose between them. Landon cleared his throat and in an attempt to banish it said, "Can I help you take your things into the house?"

She harrumphed, "I can take care of myself."

"I have no doubts about that." He watched as she wrestled her suitcase from the car, then led the way into the house and down the hall, flipping on the lights as he went. "Here's the guest room. Make yourself at home."

She tossed her suitcase on the bed.

He tried, very hard, not to think about that bed. Where she'd be sleeping. Tonight. "I-I'll go tend the horses, and then what do you say to a steak dinner?"

Her eyes rounded. She put a hand to her belly. "I am pretty hungry."

"Great. Kitchen's through here if you want something now." He shot her what he hoped was a friendly smile. "After the day you've had, you could probably use a beer. Cody keeps the fridge well stocked."

She snorted. "Hell. After the day I've had, I need to skip the beer and go straight to the whiskey."

Landon laughed. "He keeps the liquor cabinet well stocked as well." He showed her the gleaming bar in the great room. "Well, I'm heading out to the barn." He stilled as the vision of making love to Delilah in the hayloft snarled through his brain. "I should be a couple hours. Y-you're welcome to join me if you want some company."

She shot him a sardonic look.

He shrugged. "Just sayin'."

"Yeah. Thanks."

He nodded again and, with one last look, forced his legs to move. Walk away. Though what he really wanted, more than anything, was to put his mouth on her, to taste her again.

But as he made his way to the barn, a smile curled his lips.

Because he hadn't lost her forever. She was here. He was here.

And he had all night to warm her up.

* * *

When Landon went out to the barn to feed and water the horses, Delilah puttered in the kitchen, whipping up a veggie soufflé and twice-baked potatoes to go with the steak. But she only did it to keep her hands busy. Her mind was in a whirl.

Holy god. He was Landon McCoy. The hot hunk who had changed her tire and kissed her like it was the only thing he'd ever wanted do in his life was Landon McCoy. Cody's brother. She should have seen the likeness. She should have *known*.

Delilah had known Cody for years. Since college. She'd introduced him to Angie. When the two had fallen in love, Delilah had been delighted for them—and green with envy. Because Cody was one of the good ones. Practically the only decent man she'd ever met.

And he had a brother.

Panic rose in her chest.

She could barely resist Landon as it was. She'd be utterly lost if he turned out to be just like Cody.

The last thing she needed right now was another man. And a cowboy to boot.

Still, her heart fluttered when she heard him clomping up the steps to the house. He came into the kitchen all sweaty and covered with dust. She repressed the urge to leap on top of him.

His nose twitched. "Wow. What smells so good?"

"I made a soufflé. And potatoes."

He studied her for a moment, then murmured, "All that and she can cook too."

Heat rose on her cheeks and she glanced away. She had to.

"I'm going to hop in the shower, then I'll start the steaks. How does that sound?"

Oh god. Landon in the shower. Naked. A quiver skittered

through her at the thought. She tried valiantly to squelch it. And failed.

When he returned he was wearing a fresh shirt, and his hair was damp and slicked back. And he had shaved. The sharp line of his chin was smooth. Delilah decided it was probably better not to look at him at all, because he made her mouth water.

To cut the tension, she made them both a drink. He sipped his as he grilled the steak. Hers, she tossed back. Then made another.

By the time Landon brought the steaks to the dining room table, she'd had three.

He forked an enormous steak onto each plate, then served them both soufflé and potatoes. They sat across from each other and Landon lifted his glass. "To flat tires."

Delilah blinked. A laugh bubbled. Of all the things to drink to—"All right. To flat tires." She took a sip, and then got serious. Tore into her steak. The first bite made her moan. It was perfect. But Landon didn't notice her orgasmic rapture. He was busy groaning as well.

"Oh lord. This soufflé is amazing. Where did you learn to cook like this?"

Delilah shrugged. "Cookbooks?" She'd always dreamed of attending Cordon Bleu or taking a cooking class in Tuscany, but never had.

"Phenomenal. The potatoes remind me of a dish I had in Northern Italy."

Delilah stilled. Slowly, she raised her gaze. "Y-you've been to Italy?" Cowboys didn't go to Italy. Did they?

"Couple times." He took another bite and grunted. Then took another. "I studied history in college, before taking over the family ranch. It made sense to visit the cradle of civilization.

Went to Greece too."

Her mouth watered. She'd always wanted to go there as well. "So...why does a *cowboy* study history?" She just couldn't help asking. That fact was so at odds with her assumptions about his...type.

He snorted a laugh. "Because it interests me, Delilah," he said her name like a caress.

Her heart *ker-chunked*. "Do you...happen to like opera?" She held her breath as she waited for his response. *Please say no. Please say no.*

"God no."

Relief gushed through her.

"Except the arias." *Hell.* "*Pearl Fishers* is my favorite."

Oh. Hell.

"Me too." A peep.

He smiled at her, and she felt her resistance utterly drain away. Sure, he was a cowpoke, but he was a gentleman and a scholar. He liked to travel. He loved *The Pearl Fishers*.

And he smelled divine, something spicy and woodsy. Something essentially male.

Oh. She was in trouble.

He pushed back from the table with a sigh. "Wow." He chuckled. "Just wow. Best meal I've had in a long time. But..."

"But what?" She didn't mean to lean forward as she said this, but she had no power to withstand his charm. Not anymore.

His gaze warmed. "But...it was probably the company."

Her pulse surged.

"I just can't stop thinking about that kiss, Delilah. Please tell me it was phenomenal for you as well."

She should end this now. Just say no. Just open her mouth and say—

"Yes."

Awareness hummed between them; their gazes locked across the table.

"I'd like to kiss you again. But not a little kiss. And not just one." His intent scorched her. "May I?"

"Yes."

A whisper, but he heard her. His nostrils flared. "Come here."

Trembling, she stood and rounded the table. He met her halfway. Without hesitation, without pretense or pointless chatter or unnecessary seduction, he swept her into his arms and kissed her. He kissed her as though he'd been thinking about it all afternoon. As though those thoughts had deserted him, and he was left with nothing but raw simmering lust.

His kiss enflamed her, and she responded with equal fervor, pressing against him and clutching him, palming his nape and scoring his scalp with her nails in a desperate attempt to get closer. He slanted his mouth over hers, and responded in kind. Then his lips traveled over her cheek, her chin. He nested in the crook of her neck. He found a spot, the spot that lit a flame in her belly.

She groaned as he nibbled, nipped.

He pressed her back onto the table, unmindful of the clink of glasses, the clatter of silver and china as it tumbled to the floor.

"God, Delilah," he groaned as he found her breasts. "I want you so bad." He fumbled with the buttons of her blouse.

An agony of want raked through her as his knuckles scraped over her hard nipples. She gasped and arched her hips against his.

His cock was hard and thick. His need unmistakable.

He made a growling sound in his throat, practically yanked

off her bra and encased the swollen tips of her breasts in the warm cavern of his mouth. Suckled.

Shards of delight shot through her.

"Do you like this? Do you?" He nipped one bud then the other.

She opened her thighs to him, cradling his lean hips between her legs, locked her ankles around his waist, and pulled him closer. "Do it again."

He did. As he tormented her, back and forth, his hand skimmed up her bare leg to the juncture of her thighs. Nudged her clit.

A teasing touch. A featherlight whisper. But she felt it. She felt it to her core. A sizzling bolt of electrical lust. A shudder, a precursor, passed through her.

Inflamed, she reached for the band of his jeans. "Off," she snarled, a guttural command.

He kicked his way out of his jeans, frantically toeing off his boots. Her heart surged at the sight of the rigid wedge arching up his belly. Her pussy clenched when she noticed the damp spot at the tip, soaking through the cotton.

Desperation racked her. She had to see him. Tugged at his briefs. "Off. Take them off."

His magnificent cock sprang free. Impatient. Ready. She wanted to taste him, but there was no time for that. She needed him. Now. She yanked off her panties and leaned back on the table and spread her legs. "In me."

He stilled and stared at her, his eyes burning fire, Adam's apple working in his beautiful thick throat. "Oh, fuck, yeah," he mumbled, fumbling for the condom in his wallet, not taking his avid gaze from her splayed body. He tore the foil package open and slipped on the condom, and then held her in place as he slid inside her.

Delight—absolute fucking delight—scored her as he burrowed his way through her slick, swollen folds, stretching her. Filling her. Completely.

He hissed as he sank deeper, shuddered as he kissed her womb. "God, Delilah. You are so tight. So...good."

She whimpered when he eased out, but he quickly reversed direction and filled her again. "Yeah, baby. Fuck me."

His breath stalled at her command. His fingers tightened on her flesh, holding her steady on the rocking table so he could pummel her with pleasure.

Like a wild man, he plunged in, again and again. From this angle and that, in a wild frenzy that fed hers. Each rabid thrust, every savage plunge drove her higher and higher and higher until she didn't think she could bear the anguish.

And then he found it—that magical bundle of raw nerves that made her quiver and shake. His pace slowed. His angle shifted. Holding her frantic gaze, he massaged her, tormented her, stroking, rubbing, nudging at her sanity.

"Landon." A desperate plea. A whisper. A command.

"What do you want Delilah? Tell me what you need, baby."

"More. More. *More.*" She couldn't manage another word. Another thought.

He stilled inside her, buried in her, his cock thrumming with every beat of his heart. She tried to twitch her hips, make him move again, but he held her still. Impaling her. Dominating her. "Oh," he whispered, his voice a low rumble. "You want more?"

"Yes!"

"Do you like it rough? Tell me, darlin'."

"Yes."

His eyes glinted. Still he didn't move. Desperation clawed her. She was close. So close..."Landon!"

"Say please."

His expression, his tone, the very timbre of his words and what they represented sang to her. Something inside her melted, burst into flame. A shudder took her. And then another. She licked her lips.

He tracked the path of her tongue. The muscles on his neck stood out from the strain. The agony on his face was clear. "Say it," he hissed.

She couldn't resist. Couldn't hesitate or pretend. This was raw. This was bare. This was feral hunger. *"Please."*

His breath gushed out, hard and hot. Relief. And he took her, fucked her, possessed her. Like a savage he ravaged her, pounding into her quim again and again, shifting directions, thrusting here and there, plucking at her nipples and thrumming her clit as he played out a delicious operetta on her body. Her soul soared toward heaven. Reaching, clawing for it. So close. So close. So...

And then his tenor changed. The muscles of his beautiful face tightened. His strokes became shorter, harder, more frantic.

She was right there with him.

He stared at her, his eyes wild, his expression intent. He increased his thrusts. Something inside her curled, constricted. The pressure became exquisite, unbearable.

And then she broke. Rapture descended. She came in a glorious rain.

His body lurched as he found his release as well. His soul-deep moan, which sounded very much like her name, warbled through the room.

They collapsed in each other's arms.

On the table.

Amidst the remains of dinner.

After they recovered, Landon gathered her up and carried

her to the couch and simply held her. When she met his gaze, he thumbed away a stray tear and smiled. "That was amazing."

It had been. He'd been so patient and thoughtful. He'd made sure she came before he finished.

He cleared his throat. "I, um...I'd really like to do that again sometime." He stroked her hair. "Would you?"

"Yes." Oh. Yes. The hell with her trepidation about cowboys. To hell with all the jerks of the past who'd tried so hard to ruin her faith. This guy was a keeper. No matter the risks.

"Excellent." He kissed her. "Oh, and Delilah?"

"Yes Landon?"

"Whatever you do, don't tell Angie what we did on her dining room table. Okay? She'd kill me."

Delilah laughed and drew him down for another kiss. "Hmm. What will you do in exchange for my silence, cowboy?"

He grinned. Glorious dimples dented his cheeks. "I'm sure I can think of something..."

And he did.

Heaven help her, he did.

SHALL WE DANCE?

Myla Jackson

Sadie Lushbaum checked her odometer again before turning onto the gravel drive and passing beneath the arched rock and cedar gate with the words FLYING M RANCH seared into the wood. The M had to stand for McAllister. She had to be in the right place. The directions had indicated fifteen miles outside of Hole in the Wall. The sun still burned bright, beginning its slow descent to the western horizon.

"This is your chance," Audrey had assured her. "He's willing to pay you as much as you make in the entire month for one night. One lousy night. I'd do it myself, but he broke my toe at his last lesson at the Ugly Stick Saloon. If I thought I'd be of any assistance, I'd drag my ass to his place and turn cartwheels all night. The man's desperate. He promised a woman he'd dance with her at a wedding tomorrow."

"Tomorrow?" Sadie had asked. "He broke your toe at your last lesson, and you expect me to teach him how to waltz by tomorrow?"

"Honey, if you don't do it, any one of the other girls at the saloon would give their left breast to take the job. *You* saw him. Joe McAllister might have two left feet, but he's six feet six inches of gotta-love-me-some-smokin'-hot cowboy. I'm offering it to you because number one, you need the cash more than any of the others, and two, you have the patience of a saint. And I believe it might take a miracle to get him dance-worthy by tomorrow."

Sadie's heart warmed. That Audrey had that much faith in her ability to teach a hopeless man to dance said a lot. And to think, six months ago, Sadie had been resigned to the fact she'd never dance again. Funny how it took a divorce, losing her job and being flat broke to shake her out of the giant rut she'd lived in for the past ten years and get her finally chasing some of her own dreams.

"Oh, and Sadie...he's a widower."

Sadie frowned. "This isn't an attempt at matchmaking, is it? I don't need a man in my life. If you recall, the last one wasn't so great."

Audrey shrugged, a secretive smile playing on her lips. "Just sayin'. Not all men are cut out of the same cloth. You might get to give the vibrator a rest."

Audrey's words echoed in Sadie's head as she wound along the driveway beneath gnarled oak trees, emerging into the open at the base of a low hill. Perched at the top of the rise was a beautiful white limestone and cedar ranch house with a wide, shaded porch surrounding the two-story structure.

She parked and climbed out, straightening the sweeping fabric of the calf-length dress that swirled around her body when she danced. Her knees shook, and her heart beat a rapid tattoo against her ribs. Audrey had been right. Every girl who worked at the Ugly Stick had drooled over the handsome cowboy with the sexy smile and faded jeans. Sadie had been no different. She'd watched him throughout his first painful couple of lessons and cringed when his big boot crunched down on Audrey's poor toe.

After the ill-fated lesson, Sadie had gone home to her vibrator, imagining it to be Joe sliding his cock across her skin and teasing her clit into a mind-melting orgasm. A frustrating night and day later, here she was pulling up to his house. Holy shit, how was she going to look him in the eye after having imaginary sex with him, not once, but five times?

Sadie almost turned back, but she needed money for rent, and all she had in her refrigerator was a quart of sour milk and a hunk of moldy cheese. It was teach this man to dance or go home horny *and* hungry. The man had to know how to waltz to impress a woman tomorrow. Sadie couldn't let him down, nor could she jump his bones. That would be wrong, wouldn't it? The man wasn't learning to dance to impress *her*.

She mounted the steps to the door. With her hand raised to knock, she paused, fighting a panic attack.

Before she could run, the door swung open and a man called out. "Joe, get your clothes on, you've got company!" The man pushed the screen open for her. "Hi, I'm Sam, and I'd sure love to stay and watch, but I have to go milk a bull." Over his shoulder he yelled, "See ya tomorrow! And get it right this time, Joe. Mandy's countin' on you."

Sadie stepped into the cool interior of the home, wowed by the two-story, cathedral ceilings with thick cedar beams and a stone fireplace stretching from floor to ceiling on one whole wall.

"Is it the dance instructor?" Joe stepped through a doorway, wearing nothing but jeans, unbuttoned at the top. A towel draped over his head, and droplets of water glistened over his broad, muscular chest. Flinging the towel back he looked up. "Oh, you're here."

Sadie pressed a hand to her chest, her mouth suddenly dry and her pulse racing. *Wow.*

Joe glanced down at his naked chest, his cheeks flushing. "Sorry, I just got in from taking care of the horses and didn't want to smell like one." He looked up and winked.

Wow. Sadie managed to stay upright on rubbery legs.

"Sadie, isn't it?" His voice washed over her like warm wet sand, oozing into every pore.

She nodded.

He backed away. "I'll slip into a shirt, and we can get started."

"Don't get dressed on my account," she said in a gravelly whisper.

His smile broadened. "Just a shirt then. I'm not wearing my boots tonight. Hopefully you won't limp away with a broken toe." Joe disappeared and was back a moment later, his dark hair finger-combed back from his forehead. He pulled a chambray shirt over his shoulders and left the buttons loose.

Sadie feasted her gaze on his chiseled chest, her pussy tightening. When she realized she'd been staring, she dipped her head and pulled her music player and mini-portable speakers from her purse. "Shall—" she squeaked. Clearing her throat, she started again. "Shall we get started?"

He held out his hands. "I'm all yours. Teach me."

Oh, boy. For the first time since her divorce, Sadie had the wild and uncontrollable urge to throw herself at a man and beg him to make love to her. Barefoot and wearing his shirt untucked and unbuttoned down to his navel, he was the most gorgeous cowboy she'd met.

Sadie fumbled to untangle the electrical cord from the speaker wires, wondering how she'd get through this session without bursting into an orgasmic flame. "Audrey said you need to waltz at an event tomorrow."

"That's right." Big hands closed around hers, sending waves of lust shooting to her core. "Let me." He removed the items from her hands, untangled them with swift efficiency and plugged them in. Then he stood back, tucking his thumbs into his back pockets. "I'm going for a beer, would you care for one, or a glass of wine?"

"A beer would be nice." And maybe it would settle her nerves and make it easier to assume the role of teacher to this student. A thrill of challenge and something else slipped beneath her skin and rippled all the way through her body, pooling at her center.

Sadie flipped through the music, settling on a smooth, easy waltz, turning it up loud enough to be heard, but not so loud they couldn't talk over it. Then she wandered across the living room to the kitchen, the rooms separated by a wide granite bar with stools lining the front.

Joe grabbed two longnecks from the refrigerator, twisted off the tops and set one on the bar. "Here's to teaching this old dog new tricks." He lifted his bottle and downed a third of it before he set it down.

Sadie tipped hers back and swallowed an equal portion, determined to shake off the edge. "You're not old."

"Going on forty-two." He rounded the counter and stood in front of her. "And you're what, twenty-six, maybe twenty-seven?" His finger rose to touch her cheek.

"Thirty-four." Sadie blushed. "But thanks."

"Good. I'd hate for my teacher to be young enough to be my daughter." His face grew serious. "It's real important to me to learn this dance. It's a surprise for tomorrow."

"Why did you wait so long for lessons?"

"Wish I could say I was too busy herdin' cows, bailin' hay

and muckin' stalls." He shrugged. "Truth is, I haven't danced since my wife died."

"Oh?" Sadie swallowed hard. "You must have loved her very much."

"I did." He gave her a gentle smile.

Sadie's chest squeezed, and she glanced at her feet. What did she say to that?

"Life has a way of marchin' on." He lifted her chin with his finger. "That's where you come in."

Her heart fluttering, Sadie gulped. "Me?"

Joe straightened his shoulders. "As part of moving on, I promised myself that I'd learn to waltz for someone special. Problem is, I've got two left feet."

The other problem was that Sadie lusted after a man who wanted to impress another woman. Even if she wanted another man in her life, that ruled out this particular cowboy.

Sadie dug deep for the strength to teach. With a forced smile, she kicked off her shoes. "Then let's make this easy." She lifted her beer. "Finish up. It might help you be more receptive to the beat."

Together, they lifted their beers and downed them in several long gulps.

Sadie wiped her arm across her lips and then held out her hands. "Shall we?"

Joe, looking less at ease, let her guide one of his big hands to the small of her back, the other she held out and away from their bodies. He stood awkwardly away from her. "Like this?"

"It's a start." Sadie laid her hand on his shoulder. "Now close your eyes."

He did as she said.

Without his piercing blue gaze reading her every expression, Sadie could study the man up close and her focus rested on full, sensuous lips. "I'm going to sway to the beat. For now, stand there and feel how my body moves to the music."

Sadie shifted her weight from one foot to the other in time with the song. "Can you feel it?" *She* sure was.

"Not really," he admitted.

She moved his hands, placing them on her hips, her breath hitching as the warmth of his palms seared through her dress.

"That's better." His rich voice slid like warm honey over her body.

Sadie gulped. *Man, this was going to be tough.* "Sway with me," she said, her voice husky with desire.

Joe's stiff body jerked out of sync with the music. After a moment or two, he stopped and opened his eyes. "It doesn't feel the same as when you do it. Can't we skip right to the waltz? I have to be able to do that by tomorrow."

Sadie shook her head. "You have to understand the rhythm before you can master the waltz." She dropped her hands, and he dropped his as well. "Let's try something different. When I was little, my daddy taught me to dance by letting me stand on his feet. I'd move to the beat because he did."

Joe's brows twisted. "Uh, I'm too big to dance on your feet, and we both know what happens when I do."

Sadie laughed. "No, you won't dance on my toes, but you need to be close enough to move with me." She breathed deep and stepped closer, sliding her feet between his and wrapping her arms around his waist. "Now hug me."

"That's not hard to do." He wrapped her in his arms. "You smell pretty."

Sadie chuckled. "You're not so bad yourself." Then in a lust-choked voice she whispered, "Move with me."

He started out slow and jerky.

Sadie's hands moved to his ass. "Let me take the lead." She

pressed him closer until their hips moved as one. "Dancing is as natural as walking, swimming, or—"

"Riding a horse?" he offered.

"Making love." God, had she said that? Her heart raced and her body burned against his.

He pulled Sadie closer, the ridge beneath his fly more pronounced. "Makes more sense when you explain it like that."

Nothing made sense about what she was doing. But it felt right.

Through the next two songs, Sadie held him close and let him move with her to the music's rhythm. The more they swayed together, the more the soft rubbing of their bellies and chests increased, causing enough abrasion to ignite a raging inferno within her.

At the end of the second song, Sadie pushed away and pressed her hands against her cheeks. "I think you have it. Let's get to work on the waltz." This time when she assumed the correct position, with Joe's warm hand, chastely in the middle of her back, she focused on the reason for her visit.

Joe needed to waltz by tomorrow.

"I liked the other way better." His firm hand at the small of her back urged her closer.

Before she could close the distance and sink back into his embrace, Sadie reminded herself he was learning to dance for another woman. She slipped from his hands. "Hold the position."

Sadie talked him through the steps, counting through the next song until he could do it by himself, mouthing the numbers.

"The waltz was considered risqué in the eighteen-hundreds."

His lips twisted. "I'm not feeling it, dancing by myself."

"Now that you have the steps down…" She slid into his arms. "Close your eyes like before, and *feel* the three-count instead of counting."

"Feel, huh?" Again, his arms enveloped her in a warm, strong hold. "Now, you're talkin'." He closed his eyes, his body moving with hers to the three-count of the music.

He had the rhythm, his body moving to the music and in sync with hers. Heat built inside Sadie like a teakettle bubbling to a boil. The closer he held her, the hotter she blazed. Her fingers curled into his palm, clutching harder as she melted against him. Every time her breasts pressed to his chest, her nipples pebbled, and she couldn't help a quick indrawn breath. "You're getting it." *Oh, boy, was he.*

"This feels real good," he murmured against her hair. "It's kinda like postin' in the stirrups. You gotta time it right or you bust your balls."

The humor in his words broke through her sensuous trance and made her giggle. What started as a giggle, turned into a laugh, and she stopped in the middle of the floor. "Way to kill the moment."

His hands slipped down to her hips. "You felt it too?" His grip tightened, drawing her against the hard ridge beneath his jeans. "It wasn't just me?"

Her laughter dying, Sadie stared up into Joe's eyes. She shook her head, unable to voice the roiling emotions welling inside.

He smoothed a stray hair behind her ear. "I'm glad Audrey sent you. Did she tell you I stepped on her toe because I was looking at you across the room?"

"No, she didn't." Sadie's breath caught. "I didn't think you knew I existed."

"How could I miss you? You had the nicest smile of any of the waitresses or dancers at the Ugly Stick Saloon. And the prettiest red hair."

Sadie lifted a hand to her hair. "I always considered it a curse."

He wove his fingers through the strands and pulled, tugging her head back. "It's what makes you even more special."

Warmth spread up her neck and into her cheeks. "Thanks."

"I never knew dancing could be so..." He cupped her face, his mouth lowering toward hers. "...arousing...until I met you."

She skimmed her fingers across his chest, parting his shirt to find the hard muscles beneath. Electric shocks ignited at every point their bodies connected. All the naughty dreams she'd had about him rose to taunt her. "You have no idea how provocative dancing can be," she whispered.

"Like sex with your clothes on." He claimed her lips, branding her with his heat, his tongue sliding between her teeth to stroke hers.

Her senses erupted in joy, spurring her past those niggling reminders of the *other* woman. One hand slid up to the back of his neck, feathering through his crisp, dark hair. She curled her calf behind his, angling her leg upward until her crotch rode his thigh.

He grabbed the backs of her legs and wrapped them around his waist and walked with her toward a wall, where he leaned her against its hard surface. His blue gaze darkening to gray, he stared into her eyes. "You know, I didn't hire you for this. Say the word and it stops here."

Sadie chewed on her lower lip. "I didn't come here to seduce you."

His bark of laughter was short and tense. "Seduce me? Is that what you did? And here I thought I was the one seducing you. I really am out of practice. Sexy Sadie, are you up for a little *mutual* seduction?"

It was wrong. She wasn't there to make love to this man— she was there to teach him how to dance. But she couldn't deny her longing, the raging fire burning within, begging for satisfaction. Throwing sanity to the wind, she touched her lips to his. "Yes."

His mouth crashed down over hers, his fingers tugging the skirt of her dress upward until he could slip his hands underneath and cup her ass.

Sadie wiggled her bottom against his grasp, liking the way his coarse palms abraded her soft skin, and glad she'd replaced all her briefs with thong panties the day she'd signed her divorce papers.

She rocked her pussy against the denim bulge beneath her, frustrated by the barrier between her and the promise of more. Breaking off their kiss, she pressed her hands against his chest. "Stop."

Immediately his head came up and his hands released her bottom. "What?" He blinked, his eyes glazed. "Did I move too fast?"

"No. No. It's not that." She unlocked her legs from around his waist and let them slide down his thighs. "It's just…"

As her feet touched the ground, he backed up a step, running a shaking hand through his hair. "I'm sorry. I've been out of this too long."

"Me, too." Sadie laughed, her skirt drifting down around her calves. Then she twisted her fingers in the front of his shirt and leaned up on her toes, pressing a kiss to his full, sensuous lips. "And hopefully, this dance isn't over." Before he could completely close down, she slipped her hand down his chest, flicking the remaining buttons on his shirt open, continuing on to push free the button on his jeans. "Sex with your clothes on isn't nearly as fun…"

"As doing it naked." Joe caught the hem of her dress and dragged it up over her head, tossing it across a bar stool.

Standing in nothing but her thong panties, Sadie's body

quivered in anticipation of what might come next.

Joe reached into his back pocket, removed his wallet and dug out a foil packet. "I hope it's still good. It's been in there a long time," he muttered, dragging off his jeans and rolling the condom down over his shaft. He advanced toward her, naked and beautiful, the warrior hero on the path to plunder his prize. He held out his hand, a smile twitching at the corners of his lips. "Shall we dance?"

Sadie shimmied out of her panties and took his hand, delicious shivers making her body tremble and her pussy cream.

Slightly awkward at first, Joe guided her across the floor to the steps of the waltz, his cock rubbing her belly, teasing her into a lathering frenzy. Their movements coalesced until their bodies swayed as one, and they danced naked around the room. As the music softened, Joe slowed, pressing her against a wall. He gathered her close and wrapped her legs around his waist, his cock nudging her entrance. "I never knew how wonderful dancing could be." He eased into her, his lips capturing hers as he whispered, "With the right instruction."

Her channel slick with her desire, Sadie accepted him, reveling in how he filled and stretched her, driving his cock all the way into her. She dug her fingernails into his skin as tingling sensations hit her in waves, flowing through her body like a rising tide. To the beat of the music, he thrust into her, again and again, matching the rhythm perfectly.

Sadie rode the crest until she pitched over the edge, a series of explosions rocking her to the core. Her body tensed as Joe thrust one last time, holding her hips, pressing her down over him, his jaw tight, his cock pulsing inside her.

A minute, an hour, a lifetime might have passed—Sadie couldn't tell. The haze of their passion ultimately cleared. Joe slipped from inside her and let her legs slide down his body to the floor. He leaned against the wall and brushed his lips across hers. "Best dance lesson, *ever.*"

Without his skin against hers, the air-conditioned air chilled her body and jolted her back to reality. "It's getting late." She ducked beneath his arm and quickly gathered her clothing, a lump settling in her chest, tightening her throat. "You have an event to dance at tomorrow."

He reached out and grabbed her hand. "But I'm not ready."

Her gaze slipped to his still hardened manhood. "Oh, honey, you're ready."

"Please come." Joe tugged her toward him.

She resisted. "Won't the woman you're going to dance with be upset?"

He smiled. "Hardly. We've reserved the tea gardens at seven tomorrow evening. Please, say you'll be there."

Sadie shook her head. "I don't think so." She didn't think she could stand to see him dance with another woman. Especially after what they'd just shared. She pulled her dress over her head and down her hips, anxious to leave before she fell apart in front of him. When she glanced around for her panties, she couldn't see through the blur of tears in her eyes. She gave up, grabbed her purse and turned to face him. "Thank you."

He grabbed her arm and turned her toward him. "You don't have to leave, you know."

"Yes, I do." The words came out in a whisper, sound refusing to make it past her constricted vocal cords.

He tipped her chin upward. "Why are you crying?"

Was he that dense? "I have to go."

"If you change your mind about tomorrow, I'm saving a dance for you." He bent to kiss her.

Unable to turn away, her lips met his in a searing, heart-breaking kiss. For the first time since her divorce, Sadie had opened her heart and her body to a man. She melted against his naked body, wishing she was more than just a name on his dance card. Finally, she shoved her hands between them and pushed out of his embrace.

She ran from his house, flung herself into her car and jerked the shift into reverse.

Not until she'd pulled out onto the country highway did she allow the tears to fall and before long, she had to pull to the side of the road until the storm abated and she could see well enough to drive home.

Sleep didn't come to her that night and she lay in bed past noon. With her heart aching, she left a message that she wouldn't be working that night at the Ugly Stick, feigning illness. She needed the paycheck, especially since she planned on refusing Joe's payment for services rendered.

As dusk settled on Temptation, Texas, she stared at the clock. Six. Sadie's pulse quickened. At seven, Joe would be dancing in the tea garden with the woman he'd learned to waltz for. Didn't making love to her mean anything to him? Hell, she'd wasted an entire day moping over the damned cowboy.

Anger spiked inside Sadie, driving her into the shower. She applied makeup, did her hair and put on the go-to-hell red dress she'd purchased after her divorce and hadn't had the courage to wear. She had a bone to pick with a tease of a cowboy and she might as well look damned good when she did.

Cars lined the drive into the tea gardens, forcing Sadie to park half a mile away and walk in. What had forced this cowboy to take the plunge and learn to waltz? Was it the woman? She must be extraordinary to make Joe want to change. Someone he cared about deeply.

Sadie stumbled in her killer heels and came to a halt outside the gate leading into the garden. The music drifted through the hedges—a waltz. Joe would be dancing with the woman now.

Unable to stop herself, Sadie had to see who this woman was. She pushed through the gate into the tea gardens, adorned with thousands of twinkle lights. In the middle of a makeshift wooden dance floor was Joe wearing a black tuxedo. He was so handsome it made Sadie's heart twist. In his arms was a young woman in a long white wedding dress—and he was leading her in a waltz.

Pain stabbed Sadie in her heart. She'd stumbled into a wedding. Joe's wedding?

The music faded out and another tune struck up. A young man in another black tuxedo tapped Joe's shoulder. Joe kissed the young woman on the forehead and handed her off to the other man. "Take care of her, she's all the family I have."

The young woman leaned up on her toes and kissed Joe's cheek. "I love you, Daddy."

Daddy.

Sadie's pulse fluttered and her hopes soared. He'd learned to dance for his *daughter.*

The young man kissed his bride and they danced away, leaving Joe standing on the edge of the dance floor, his gaze following the newlyweds, his face sad.

Gathering her courage, while playing down her joy, Sadie stepped up to Joe and tapped his shoulder.

He turned to her, his face lighting up. "You came."

Sadie laughed. "And not too soon, I think." She held out her hand, hope and happiness flowing from her fingertips. "Shall we dance?"

ABOUT THE AUTHORS

RANDI ALEXANDER is published with The Wild Rose Press Cowboy Kink line and Cleis Press. When she's not dreaming of, or writing about, kinky cowboys, she's biking trails along remote rivers, snorkeling the Gulf of Mexico or practicing her drumming in hopes of someday forming a tropical-rock band.

CHEYENNE BLUE's erotica has appeared in over seventy anthologies, including: *Best Women's Erotica*, *Cowboy Lust*, *Best Lesbian Romance*, *Lesbian Lust* and *Frenzy: 60 Stories of Sudden Sex*. She lives and writes by the beach in Queensland, Australia.

MICHAEL BRACKEN, writer of fiction, nonfiction and advertising copy, is the author of almost nine-hundred short stories, several of which have appeared in Cleis Press anthologies.

LAYLA CHASE, on a dare from a close friend, challenged

herself to explore the steamier side of romance and discovered all sorts of characters whose stories needed sharing. She writes contemporary and historical stories from her mountain home in California that she shares with her longtime husband and two dogs.

CYNTHIA D'ALBA started writing on a challenge from her husband and discovered having imaginary sex with lots of hunky men was fun. Her first book, *Texas Two Step*, was released in 2012 and became a publisher best seller.

SHOSHANNA EVERS is a critically acclaimed, best-selling romance author. She is published with Simon & Schuster/Gallery, Ellora's Cave, and Penguin/Berkley Heat (Agony/Ecstasy), and her work is in several Cleis Press anthologies (including *Best Bondage Erotica 2012* and *2013*). She lives in Los Angeles with her family and two big dogs.

MIA HOPKINS is a Los Angeles–based writer of romance and erotic fiction. Her work has appeared in Clean Sheets and will be featured in the forthcoming Circlet Press anthology *Under Cover of Darkness*. She was born in the year of the horse, which may explain her special fondness for cowboys.

MYLA JACKSON spent twenty years livin' and lovin' in South Texas, ranching horses, cattle, goats, ostriches and emus. A former IT professional, Myla happily writes full time, penning adventures that keep her readers begging for more. When she's not writing, she's traveling, snow-skiing, boating or riding her ATV, while concocting new stories.

EMMA JAY has been writing longer than she'd care to admit, using her endless string of celebrity crushes as inspiration for her heroes. Married twenty-six years, Emma believes writing romance is like falling in love, over and over again. Creating characters and love stories is an addiction she has no intention of breaking.

CAT JOHNSON is a self-proclaimed promo ho known for her creative marketing and research. She's sponsored bull-riding rodeo cowboys, owns a collection of cowboy boots and camouflage shoes for book signings and a number of her consultants wear combat or cowboy boots for a living.

AMBER LIN writes erotic romance with damaged souls and deep emotion. *RT Book Reviews* called her debut novel "truly extraordinary." Her latest book, a small-town romance, released in late 2013.

ROBIE MADISON pursues her own adventures traveling around the world. When she's at home, she writes about men and women who aren't afraid to take risks for love. When she's not traveling or writing, she can often be found teaching writing courses online.

MEGAN MITCHAM was a true Southern bell until she discovered the delicious world of erotic romance. Now she pens racy romances to please a reader's heart, mind and body.

SABRINA YORK, Her Royal Hotness, writes naked erotic fiction for fans who like it hot, hard and balls-to-the-wall, and erotic romance and fantasy for readers who prefer a slow burn to passion. Sabrina loves writing hot, humorous stories in multiple genres for smart and sexy readers.

ABOUT
THE EDITOR

DELILAH DEVLIN is a *USA Today* bestselling author of erotica and erotic romance with a rapidly expanding reputation for writing deliciously edgy stories with complex characters. She has published over a 120 erotic stories in multiple genres and lengths, and she is published by Atria/Strebor, Avon, Berkley, Black Lace, Cleis Press, Ellora's Cave, Harlequin Spice, HarperCollins: Mischief, Kensington, Running Press and Samhain Publishing. In January 2013, she added Montlake Romance to her list of publishers when *Shattered Souls* and *Lost Souls* released!

Her short stories have appeared in multiple Cleis Press collections, including *Lesbian Cowboys, Girl Crush, Fairy Tale Lust, Lesbian Lust, Passion, Lesbian Cops, Dream Lover, Carnal Machines, Best Erotic Romance 2012, Suite Encounters, Girl Fever, Girls Who Score, Duty and Desire* and *Best Lesbian Romance 2013*. For Cleis Press, she edited 2011's *Girls Who Bite*, and 2012's *She Shifters* and *Cowboy Lust*. In 2013, she added *Smokin' Hot Firemen* and *High Octane Heroes*.

More from Delilah Devlin

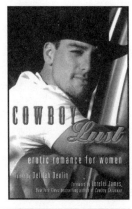

Cowboy Lust
Erotic Romance for Women
Edited by Delilah Devlin

There's a reason Western romance never goes out of fashion—cowboys are undeniably sexy. "*Cowboy Lust* is a bevy of hot, hard cowboys ready to give you more than an eight-second ride. Believe me, you don't want to miss this collection."
—Beth Williamson, author of *Hell for Leather*
ISBN 978-1-57344-814-7 $15.95

Smokin' Hot Firemen
Erotic Romance Stories for Women
Edited by Delilah Devlin

"Firefighters are damned sexy. Live vicariously and read all about their brave, gorgeous selves in Delilah Devlin's rapturous romance collection. Get your fire hose ready in case these guys get just a little too hot to handle."
—Jo Davis, bestselling author of the *Firefighters of Station Five* series
ISBN 978-1-57344-934-2 $15.95

She Shifters
Lesbian Paranormal Erotica
Edited by Delilah Devlin

"The always exhilarating author Delilah Devlin knows exactly what her readers want—daring, erotic, and wickedly delightful stories filled with amazing characters, exciting story lines, passion, and an abundance of emotions that will keep them riveted to the pages."
—The Romance Studio
ISBN 978-1-57344-796-6 $15.95

High-Octane Heroes
Erotic Romance for Women
Edited by Delilah Devlin

One glance and your heart will melt—these chiseled, brave men will ignite your fantasies with their courage and charisma. This set of smoldering-hot adventures has an intensity that leaps off the page as "super-alpha" heroes risk their lives to protect and cherish those in need.
ISBN 978-1-57344-981-6 $15.95

Many More Than Fifty Shades of Erotica

Buy 4 books, Get 1 *FREE* *

Please, Sir
Erotic Stories of Female Submission
Edited by Rachel Kramer Bussel

If you liked *Fifty Shades of Grey,* you'll love the explosive stories of *Please, Sir.* These damsels delight in the pleasures of taking risks to be rewarded by the men who know their deepest desires. Find out why nothing is as hot as the power of the words "Please, Sir."
ISBN 978-1-57344-389-0 $14.95

Yes, Sir
Erotic Stories of Female Submission
Edited by Rachel Kramer Bussel

Bound, gagged or spanked—or controlled with just a glance—these lucky women experience the breathtaking thrills of sexual submission. *Yes, Sir* shows that pleasure is best when dispensed by a firm hand.
ISBN 978-1-57344-310-4 $15.95

He's on Top
Erotic Stories of Male Dominance and Female Submission
Edited by Rachel Kramer Bussel

As true tops, the bossy hunks in these stories understand that BDSM is about exulting in power that is freely yielded. These kinky stories celebrate women who know exactly what they want.
ISBN 978-1-57344-270-1 $14.95

Best Bondage Erotica 2013
Edited by Rachel Kramer Bussel

Let *Best Bondage Erotica 2013* be your kinky playbook to erotic restraint—from silk ties and rope to shiny cuffs, blindfolds and so much more. These stories of forbidden desire will captivate, shock and arouse you.
ISBN 978-1-57344-897-0 $15.95

Luscious
Stories of Anal Eroticism
Edited by Alison Tyler

Discover all the erotic possibilities that exist between the sheets and between the cheeks in this daring collection. "Alison Tyler is an author to rely on for steamy, sexy page turners! Try her!"—Powell's Books
ISBN 978-1-57344-760-7 $15.95

Happy Endings Forever And Ever

Dark Secret Love
A Story of Submission
By Alison Tyler

Inspired by her own BDSM exploits and private diaries, Alison Tyler draws on twenty-five years of penning sultry stories to create a scorchingly hot work of fiction, a memoir-inspired novel with reality at its core. A modern-day *Story of O*, a *9 1/2 Weeks*-style journey fueled by lust, longing and the search for true love.
ISBN 978-1-57344-956-4 $16.95

High-Octane Heroes
Erotic Romance for Women
Edited by Delilah Devlin

One glance and your heart will melt—these chiseled, brave men will ignite your fantasies with their courage and charisma. Award-winning romance writer Delilah Devlin has gathered stories of hunky, red-blooded guys who enter danger zones in the name of duty, honor, country and even love.
ISBN 978-1-57344-969-4 $15.95

Duty and Desire
Military Erotic Romance
Edited by Kristina Wright

The only thing stronger than the call of duty is the call of desire. *Duty and Desire* enlists a team of hot-blooded men and women from every branch of the military who serve their country and follow their hearts.
ISBN 978-1-57344-823-9 $15.95

Smokin' Hot Firemen
Erotic Romance Stories for Women
Edited by Delilah Devlin

Delilah delivers tales of these courageous men breaking down doors to steal readers' hearts! *Smokin' Hot Firemen* imagines the romantic possibilities of being held against a massively muscled chest by a man whose mission is to save lives and serve *every* need.
ISBN 978-1-57344-934-2 $15.95

Only You
Erotic Romance for Women
Edited by Rachel Kramer Bussel

Only You is full of tenderness, raw passion, love, longing and the many emotions that kindle true romance. The couples in *Only You* test the boundaries of their love to make their relationships stronger.
ISBN 978-1-57344-909-0 $15.95

Unleash Your Favorite Fantasies

The Big Book of Bondage
Sexy Tales of Erotic Restraint
Edited by Alison Tyler

Nobody likes bondage more than editrix Alison Tyler, who is fascinated with the ecstasies of giving up, giving in, and entrusting one's pleasure (and pain) into the hands of another. Delve into a world of unrestrained passion, where heart-stopping dynamics will thrill and inspire you.
ISBN 978-1-57344-907-6 $15.95

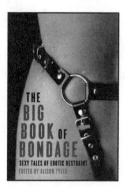

Hurts So Good
Unrestrained Erotica
Edited by Alison Tyler

Intricately secured by ropes, locked in handcuffs or bound simply by a lover's command, the characters of *Hurts So Good* find themselves in the throes of pleasurable restraint in this indispensible collection by prolific, award-winning editor Alison Tyler.
ISBN 978-1-57344-723-2 $14.95

Caught Looking
Erotic Tales of Voyeurs and Exhibitionists
Edited by Alison Tyler
and Rachel Kramer Bussel

These scintillating fantasies take the reader inside a world where people get to show off, watch, and feel the vicarious thrill of sex times two, their erotic power multiplied by the eyes of another.
ISBN 978-1-57344-256-5 $14.95

Hide and Seek
Erotic Tales of Voyeurs and Exhibitionists
Edited by Rachel Kramer Bussel
and Alison Tyler

Whether putting on a deliberate show for an eager audience or peeking into the hidden sex lives of their neighbors, these show-offs and shy types go all out in their quest for the perfect peep show.
ISBN 978-1-57344-419-4 $14.95

One Night Only
Erotic Encounters
Edited by Violet Blue

"Passion and lust play by different rules in *One Night Only*. These are stories about what happens when we have just that one opportunity to ask for what we want—and we take it… Enjoy the adventure."
—Violet Blue
ISBN 978-1-57344-756-0 $14.95

Fuel Your Fantasies

Carnal Machines
Steampunk Erotica
Edited by D. L. King

In this decadent fusing of technology and romance, outstanding contemporary erotica writers use the enthralling possibilities of the 19th-century steam age to tease and titillate.
ISBN 978-1-57344-654-9 $14.95

The Sweetest Kiss
Ravishing Vampire Erotica
Edited by D. L. King

These sanguine tales give new meaning to the term "dead sexy" and feature beautiful bloodsuckers whose desires go far beyond blood.
ISBN 978-1-57344-371-5 $15.95

The Handsome Prince
Gay Erotic Romance
Edited by Neil Plakcy

A bawdy collection of bedtime stories brimming with classic fairy tale characters, reimagined and recast for any man who has dreamt of the day his prince will come. These sexy stories fuel fantasies and remind us all of the power of true romance.
ISBN 978-1-57344-659-4 $14.95

Daughters of Darkness
Lesbian Vampire Tales
Edited by Pam Keesey

"A tribute to the sexually aggressive woman and her archetypal roles, from nurturing goddess to dangerous predator."
—*The Advocate*
ISBN 978-1-57344-233-6 $14.95

Dark Angels
Lesbian Vampire Erotica
Edited by Pam Keesey

Dark Angels collects tales of lesbian vampires, the quintessential bad girls, archetypes of passion and terror. These tales of desire are so sharply erotic you'll swear you've been bitten!
ISBN 978-1-57344-252-7 $13.95

Out of This World Romance

Steamlust
Steampunk Erotic Romance
Edited by Kristina Wright

Shiny brass and crushed velvet; mechanical inventions and romantic conventions; sexual fantasy and kinky fetish: this is a lush and fantastical world of women-centered stories and romantic scenarios, a first for steampunk fiction.
ISBN 978-1-57344-721-8 $14.95

The Sweetest Kiss
Ravishing Vampire Erotica
Edited by D. L. King

These sanguine tales give new meaning to the term "dead sexy" and feature beautiful bloodsuckers whose desires go far beyond blood.
ISBN 978-1-57344-371-5 $15.95

Dream Lover
Paranormal Tales of Erotic Romance
Edited by Kristina Wright

A potent potion of fun and sexy tales filled with male fairies and clairvoyant scientists, as well as darkly erotic tales of ghosts, shapeshifters and possession.
ISBN 978-1-57344-655-6 $14.95

Fairy Tale Lust
Erotic Fantasies for Women
Edited by Kristina Wright

Award-winning novelist and erotica writer Kristina Wright goes over the river and through the woods to find the sexiest fairy tales ever written.
ISBN 978-1-57344-397-5 $14.95

In Sleeping Beauty's Bed
Erotic Fairy Tales
By Mitzi Szereto

"Who can resist the erotic origins of fairy tales from Little Red to Rapunzel's long braid? Szereto knows her way around the mythic scholarship and the most outrageous sexual deviations in Pandora's Box."
—Susie Bright
ISBN 978-1-57344-367-8 $16.95

Best Erotica Series

"Gets racier every year."—*San Francisco Bay Guardian*

Buy 4 books,
Get 1 *FREE**

Best Women's Erotica 2013
Edited by Violet Blue
ISBN 978-1-57344-898-7 $15.95

Best Women's Erotica 2012
Edited by Violet Blue
ISBN 978-1-57344-755-3 $15.95

Best Women's Erotica 2011
Edited by Violet Blue
ISBN 978-1-57344-423-1 $15.95

Best Bondage Erotica 2013
Edited by Rachel Kramer Bussel
ISBN 978-1-57344-897-0 $15.95

Best Bondage Erotica 2012
Edited by Rachel Kramer Bussel
ISBN 978-1-57344-754-6 $15.95

Best Bondage Erotica 2011
Edited by Rachel Kramer Bussel
ISBN 978-1-57344-426-2 $15.95

Best Lesbian Erotica 2013
Edited by Kathleen Warnock.
Selected and introduced by
Jewelle Gomez.
ISBN 978-1-57344-896-3 $15.95

Best Lesbian Erotica 2012
Edited by Kathleen Warnock.
Selected and introduced by
Sinclair Sexsmith.
ISBN 978-1-57344-752-2 $15.95

Best Lesbian Erotica 2011
Edited by Kathleen Warnock.
Selected and introduced by Lea DeLaria.
ISBN 978-1-57344-425-5 $15.95

Best Gay Erotica 2013
Edited by Richard Labonté.
Selected and introduced by Paul Russell.
ISBN 978-1-57344-895-6 $15.95

Best Gay Erotica 2012
Edited by Richard Labonté.
Selected and introduced by
Larry Duplechan.
ISBN 978-1-57344-753-9 $15.95

Best Gay Erotica 2011
Edited by Richard Labonté.
Selected and introduced by
Kevin Killian.
ISBN 978-1-57344-424-8 $15.95

Best Fetish Erotica
Edited by Cara Bruce
ISBN 978-1-57344-355-5 $15.95

Best Bisexual Women's Erotica
Edited by Cara Bruce
ISBN 978-1-57344-320-3 $15.95

Best Lesbian Bondage Erotica
Edited by Tristan Taormino
ISBN 978-1-57344-287-9 $16.95

* Free book of equal or lesser value. Shipping and applicable sales tax extra.
Cleis Press • (800) 780-2279 • orders@cleispress.com
www.cleispress.com

Ordering is easy! Call us toll free or fax us to place your MC/VISA order.
You can also mail the order form below with payment to:
Cleis Press, 2246 Sixth St., Berkeley, CA 94710.

ORDER FORM

QTY	TITLE	PRICE

SUBTOTAL _____

SHIPPING _____

SALES TAX _____

TOTAL _____

Add $3.95 postage/handling for the first book ordered and $1.00 for each additional book. Outside North America, please contact us for shipping rates. California residents add 9% sales tax. Payment in U.S. dollars only.

* Free book of equal or lesser value. Shipping and applicable sales tax extra.

Cleis Press • Phone: (800) 780-2279 • Fax: (510) 845-8001
orders@cleispress.com • www.cleispress.com
You'll find more great books on our website

Follow us on Twitter @cleispress • Friend/fan us on Facebook